OTHER PUBLICATIONS

Lilibat Belly Place   ISBN No. 978-1-4678-9618-4

Phillipa is a young girl that by mistake stumbles into the world of fantasy, expectation, and magic on this small island. For children

Lilibat Lilly-Bell Place   ISBN NO. 978-1-4678-9659-7

Phillipa has a daughter Lilly-Bell who follows in her footprints. UN-be- known to her, she is part of the magic and fantasy, whether she likes it or not.

IT'S A SECRET   ISBN No. 978-1-4969-7981-0

This is a fast moving, filthy, bloody, erotic, mystery thriller. The prostitutionalised eroticism takes place in Warwickshire, Mauritius, Greece and anywhere that takes their fancy. The victims are endless and the horror is prevalent.

JEFF THE MAVERICK PECKER

WRITTEN BY

Jayne Belinda Allen

authorHOUSE®

AuthorHouse™ UK Ltd.
1663 Liberty Drive
Bloomington, IN 47403 USA
www.authorhouse.co.uk
Phone: 0800.197.4150

Published by AuthorHouse   09/15/2014

ISBN: 978-1-4969-8829-4 (sc)
ISBN: 978-1-4969-8830-0 (e)

Any people depicted in stock imagery provided by Thinkstock are models, and such images are being used for illustrative purposes only.
Certain stock imagery © Thinkstock.

This book is printed on acid-free paper.

To
My son
Simon, I
Dedicate this
Creation to him Just
because he is full of
fun, cheeky, crazy,
and dashingly
Handsome.
Love You
Son
X

A LITTLE BIOGRAPHY OF THE AUTHOR

The idea, concept, and creation came from the author's wonderful husband, Mr William John Allen. He gave her the job of bringing the characters alive. Between them, they had many hours of laughter, giggling in the tent on holiday about the next chapter and revelling in what Jeff and Hedgy were going to do next. Also, over a pint in The Fox in Attleborough, Nuneaton. The best story ideas came from sober and drunken states looking through the bottom of an empty vessel, waiting to be filled with Arh, nectar.

Jayne Belinda Allen was born in Crickowell, Wales in 1958. Her father was in the Army and so travelled to many parts of the world. Her sister was born in Hong Kong and her brothers were born in different places in England.

She went to many schools in her lifetime. From the age of ten, she studied at Haig school in Germany, Kiwi School in Salisbury England, Woodlands junior school in Chelmsley wood England, Kingshurst High School England, Atherstone High School England, Great Barr Comprehensive School in Birmingham, and Ryland

Bedford High School in Sutton Coldfield, England. She actually achieved some qualifications to boot. In her teens, she studied at Walsall Art College England. As time went by, she also studied at Walsall Technology College, Bourneville College Birmingham, and South Birmingham College.

Her thirst for writing became apparent when she was voted in as Public Relations Officer for Walsall Synchronized Swimming Club. She wrote monthly newsletters and kept the local newspapers up to date with the Synchronized swimming competition results. She also promoted the Club in local libraries across the West Midlands and the Club awarded a trophy for her outstanding work.

Jayne has worked in bookkeeping as a starter profession and then for many decades in the caring profession. She then moved to being a Senior Physiotherapy Assistant to mental health support worker. She has also worked in the voluntary sector and achieved a Synchronized Swimming Assistant Teachers Certificate, as well as lifeguard Certificate to help with the Club. She also volunteered as a book Reader, creative writing teacher and ran competitions for young children at Baddesley Ensor village hall, Atherstone, which she absolutely loved.

Her poems have been entered into anthologies and won prizes. Her art work to date, including her embroidery and craft creations have won many prizes, mostly first and the occasional second and third in the Nuneaton Festival of Arts.

She has two grown up children and a granddaughter. She re-married in 2008 to a wonderful, supportive, caring man, Mr William John Allen who is her soul mate. She presently resides in Warwickshire but time will tell if she will stay. It could be the gypsy in her. Her life has led her to many places and she has experienced the good, the bad, and the ugly in her lifetime and still smiling.

PREAMBLE

Jeff is a victim of circumstance. His fate leads him to so many different adventures. He flies, he swims, he races and slides from one fascinating horror to other fascinating venues. He lives life to the full and has an unusual friend that takes him everywhere. He meets creatures from all occupations and interacts with all who purvey his world.

His world is so naturally funny, dangerous, heart breaking, moving, exciting, sexually erotic, and educational. FOR ADULTS ONLY!

CONTENTS

IN THE BEGINNING

The sound of sirens could be heard approaching; Police, Fire, and Ambulance crews were hurtling to the scene of the accident.

Jeff Cousins had left work late and was driving a little too quickly on the winding lanes near his Berkshire home in an attempt not to miss the start of the football match he was eager to see. A fox darted out in front of him and he instinctively swung the steering wheel to the left to try to avoid it, his car was split in two by a huge Oak tree and Jeff's life was ebbing away from him.

The Police were the first to arrive and quickly closed the road off, they offered words of reassurance to Jeff, but they all knew what the outcome would be.

The Fire Brigade and Ambulance arrived around the same time, the Paramedics quickly administered pain relief to Jeff who was screaming in agony, and the Firemen prepared their cutting equipment ready to try to release him from the tangled wreckage. It was about twenty minutes before Jeff's body was removed and put in the back of the ambulance, it was then that one of the Paramedics shouted to all of his emergency colleagues, 'search the area thoroughly guys this chap has had his penis ripped off in the accident'.

Jeff's penis was lying in a ditch. The penis woke up with a stabbing pain in his side, thinking to himself, 'I thought I was the only prick around here.'

He suddenly felt himself stretching. Jeff had landed on a curled up Hedgehog and now the creature was starting to unravel itself. The hedgehog wondered what had hit him.

'Fuck me,' said the hedgehog in shock, 'Where did you come from?'

'My owner was in a car crash and I was ripped off him and landed on you, another prick, ha, ha, ha.'

A large, hairy spider bit Jeff on his shaft and injected venom into his blood stream. This had unusual properties that made Jeff feel a little woozy, to say the least. The spider cocooned Jeff and the Hedgehog both together and the spider bit Jeff again. After a short struggle, they managed to break free although this also meant they were truly stuck together. Both the hedgehog and Jeff realised that they could communicate through thought. Jeff felt pressure around the lip of his penis. He thought he must be getting some boils, side by side, and then suddenly he could see. It was not clear to start but as the day went on, Jeff became used to his new eyes. They were sore and very new. The hedgehog and Jeff read each other's thoughts, and so their journey began.

The hedgehog became infused with Jeff because of the chemicals that the spider injected into him. When the hedgehog ate something, like a worm, it also instantly fed Jeff. Jeff, after a few short yards of walking with the hedgehog connection noticed his temperament changed and he felt very happy go lucky one minute and when he spotted an obstacle that they had to climb, he then became extremely anxious, moody and downright grumpy. He also noticed that after a few miles Jeff's mood changed from sexual to mood swings, anger and so on.

In parts of this forest, the grass was almost as tall as Jeff. He could see water up ahead. Suddenly a Mallards beak engulfed Jeff.

Jeff shouted, 'steady on, it's far too early for a blow job. Put me down.'

The Mallard started chomping on Jeff's bell end. Jeff wriggled like a worm to try to free them but to no avail. The duck just gripped his beak tighter and tighter. Hedgy could feel something pulling at one of his tiny legs. He too started to wriggle. A fight broke out and dinner became a competition. Hedgy was pulled one way and Jeff the other. The intensity of the fight became scarily worse, and then freedom was apparent. Jeff and Hedgy hurtled through the air, scarily not knowing where they were going to land, how they were going to hit the ground, and what they were flying into. Duff, bang, splat, the decking of a Narrow boat was underneath them. It was a bloody hard surface to hit at a hundred miles an hour, no a thousand miles per hour. 'Ouch,' screamed both.

Luckily for both, Hedgy had landed on his tiny paws and managed to balance Jeff at the same time. They both adjusted their position and just stood there like statues to catch their breaths and to find out where, what, and how they were going to get off this sailing vessel.

Jeff saw a young woman's bum staring at him. She was dressed but had no knickers on. She grabbed a pair off her washing line and the boat shuddered. She lost her balance and sat on Jeff. Jeff realised the daylight had gone. The pitch was familiar and the soft, wet warmth engulfed his senses. I know this place. I love this place. Hedgy shuffled in panic from side to side. The woman sat there for a moment and when Hedgy moved, she liked it. Jeff said, 'come on put your back into it. This woman is enjoying this and so am I. Wahoo, dance Hedgy, dance.'

'You try moving with ten ton Tess sitting on top of you.'

'If you don't she will find out about us, so wriggle, bump and grind as if your life depended on it.'

'Ok, ok, I'm trying, I'm bumping and grinding.'

'Oh yeah, oh wow, oh more.'

'I'm going as fast as I can. You try doing this. It ain't easy.'

Jeff was in happy land. He had landed in his favourite place of all time and somebody was doing all the hard work for a change. Paradise, he revelled, paradise.

Inside got tighter and tighter until Jeff excreted his favourite medicine, Sperm for the woman he thought, oh yes, and a blast from the past. He went limp and passed out. The overwhelming sensation was just too much. The woman after her pleasures looked down at Hedgy and screamed. She got hold of Jeff by his bell end, and threw him over board.

Again, they both hurtled into the air. Hedgy was disorientated and extremely scared to death, almost. Splash, both hit the water. Hedgy had never swum before and the cold woke the loins of Jeff up. He tried to take a deep breath, but swallowed gallons of water. Hedgy tried to scramble to the surface but Jeff was far too heavy. Jeff was making Hedgy turn on his back. Finally, Hedgy managed to scoop himself to the surface but he was upside down. He screamed at Jeff, 'you're going have to get off. I can't breathe, I can't swim, and you are holding us under. You're killing me.'

Jeff screamed back, 'move your legs, and paddle. Do a circular movement with your legs to go one way.'

Hedgy did as he was told, at the same time shouted at Jeff to get the hell off him. He'd had enough of carrying him.

Jeff suddenly found he was in the dark again but it felt a little painful, especially around his knob. His eyes had been cleaned and the good news was, he could see much better, with clarity. He was drained from his prior performance and realised he could, should, would not do it again. He wondered how they were going to get out of this one. Hedgy was frantic, traumatised and could see the sky from the shear throw of them both through the air again. Hedgy saw a huge fish holding onto Jeff with a fishing line attached, it was a huge ugly looking Pike. Hedgy could also see a very old angler trying to pull in his line that was stretched to the mouth of the fish. With the pull of the line, the fish had no choice but to let go of Jeff to try to save his own life. Hedgy and Jeff with freedom in hand, bounced off the edge of the canals soft-grassed bank and then gambolled down an embankment out of sight.

BATTERED, BRUISED AND NOWHERE TO GO

Battered and bruised, painfully motionless, they lay there, soaking up the stillness. The sheer delight of touching the ground was calming and relieving. They just laid there looking at the sky. It was a comfortably warm, grass meadow. Jeff closed his eyes after the relaxation hit all his being and he succumbed to melting into relief. Hedgy said nothing. He too was overwhelmed with just not moving.

Jeff woke up cold. The warm day had turned to a biting chilly evening. In the undergrowth, they were duveted with foliage on all sides, which helped the intensity of the drafts. Hedgy moved slightly to get a better position for one of his tiny legs that had been squashed to numbness. He jiggered to the irritation of pins and needles in his back toes. Jeff got angry and told him to keep still because every time Jeff moved he could feel every hurt that had been inflicted on him in the middle of the day.

Jeff heard rustling. Movement from the left was getting louder, closer and frightfully scarier with every breath.

Hedgy sat as a statue and sent, 'what the hell was that,' messages to Jeff.

A rat that looked over Jeff's bell end and darted past to catch a vole for his supper approached them. He threw his body over Jeff and caught his prey. As quick as he came, as quickly he went. They could hear weird noises, owls hooting, things shuffling. Things were crawling over them as their muscles froze, so as not to be felt, seen, or heard. Hedgy's thought was, there is nowhere safe for us?'

They both agreed that if they stayed where they were, it would be only time before they were eaten alive. It was time to move on, but slowly, very slowly. As they moved, they realised their aches and pains went with every motion. Hedgy saw a flat surface and realised it was a tarmacked path. It was smoother for their aches and pains to glide with the least amount of traction.

As time moved on so did the pains of escape. Eventually the rhythm and motion flexed their muscles and became easier to manoeuvre.

After a mile or two, they spotted a dilapidated shed or barn. Either way it looked a dam site safer than from whence they came.

Jeff said quietly and tiredly, 'shall we stop here then?'

Hedgy replied exhausted, 'yeah, jump off.'

'You know I can't do that. Just take a chill pill. That corner over there looks safe for now.'

Hedgy was fed up already of carrying Jeff and retorted, 'you're too heavy. Just get off my back, will ya. You're killing me?'

Jeff was in no mood for arguing and totally ignored Hedgy's grumbles. He fell down and Hedgy hit the deck floor sideways. He was just about to give another mouthful to Hedgy, when he just told him to sleep. Hedgy was just about to gripe when he ended up just listening and agreed to, just sleep.

NO PEACE FOR THE WICKED

Morning rain chucked it down. The leaky roof dripped globules of water on their bodies. They were cold, uncomfortable and bemused as to how they both ended up the way they had. It was a question of circumstance and a judgement call for both of them.

Hedgy demanded, 'ok, the games over. I want you off my back for good. I want my life back. I have friends in high places that would do you over just for the hell of it.'

'Ok, what ya gonna do about it. I'm stuck to your stupid back and welded to your stupid spiny things. How the hell are you going to separate us. I would love to get back to my body and be so called, normal again. To be quite honest life was so much easier. You get your mates and get me off you.'

'Hang on. Where are we? I've never been to this neck of the woods.'

'You're lucky, I've only ever seen daylight a few times in my life, so no I don't know where the fuck we are. You are asking the wrong dick.'

'Ok, right. Let's try and find somebody who can help us get away from each other then'

'Whhoooopppppeeeee, we have a plan. Who, where, what are we going to do then?'

Hedgy prized his body up and heaved with all his might to get to his feet. Jeff obliged by trying to swing forward and balanced his weight for the purpose of moving forward. It worked. Both were standing and ready to find a solution to their problems.

Hedgy decided to prioritise first things first and eat something. His belly was rumbling and whatever he ate also fed Jeff. He was very good at chasing worms and then pulling them out of the ground. He spotted one. He dug his nose in the soil until he could feel the flesh of his prey. He bit the nose of the worm and pulled. A little, at a time, the worm stretched to the surface and Hedgy quickly gripped it until he had half the worm's body clamped in his teeth. One more big pull and he had the soft wriggly skin in his mouth, chomping away until it was no more. Jeff decided he just could not look at what Hedgy was doing because he found it revolting, to say the least. Jeff started to wretch and deliberately asked Hedgy to try to find some bread because he liked bread.

Hedgy replied sarcastically, 'yeah, right, I will just go to the local shops and get you a couple of loaves. You just wait here.'

Jeff replied indignantly, 'very good. In addition, don't forget the dog food for you. Woof, Woof!'

Hedgy ignored him and pulled a few more worms to munch whilst Jeff tried not to watch. Hedgy eventually became satisfied with his feast and trotted more comfortably along the meadow-grassed path.

A woman of petite stature trotted with a tiny Chihuahua dog. He had his nose up in the air smelling the scent of adventure. He tasted Hedgy and could not quite work out what was on his body. The dog stood to attention and the woman followed. The dog then pulled her vigorously towards Hedgy and tried to bite his little shins.

The woman screamed, 'Rocky, stop that. Rocky, no.'

Hedgy screeched and tried to get away. Unfortunately, for them both, the woman took note of Jeff on the top of Hedgy and her eyes analysed this strange looking overgrowth on the hedgehog's spikes. She instantly jumped to the conclusion that the hedgehog had got a cancerous growth and needed medical attention right away. She thought she could save an animal in distress by taking control and curing his illness. With that thought, she took from her pocket one of those pooh bags for dog shite and covered Jeff and Hedgy fully in white plastic. They tried struggling but the straps held firmly and the plastic was quite strong. One of Hedgy's legs was dangling out of the bag and the dog tried to bite it. Fortunately, the woman had the decency to manipulate his leg into a safer place and put a breathing hole, pierced at the bottom of the bag for Hedgy.

The first thing she did was seemingly walk forever to her home, which incidentally was roughly two miles away from where they were discovered. The Chihuahua would not leave the pair alone. He kept on jumping up at the plastic container holding Jeff and Hedgy all the way home. Jeff thought, that woman has a lot of patience to have a dipstick like that for a friend. Eventually, they arrived and the contents of the bag, namely Jeff and Hedgy were dropped into a large round Tupperware container. This time the husband of the woman stared straight at Jeff and Jeff wriggled to hit him on the head. The man said in horror, 'that's not a tumour that's alive. It moved. It tried to kick me and it looks like a Penis.'

'What D'you mean it kicked you? It's some kind of growth, not a penis. You stupid man. Get away. I am going to take it to our vets.'

'Whatever. I tell you it's alive and kicking.'

'Out of my way. Talk to you later.'

With that, she took the container and contents and drove to her nearest vets, without the Chihuahua.

She went in and registered her problem. She must have waited at least an hour and a half and then she heard the vet ask her to go into a private room. She smiled and followed. When she got into the small room, she put the container on the table. The vet peered into it and was amazed and puzzled as to what she saw. She said, 'it looks like a human penis attached to a hedgehog.'

'Don't be stupid. It can't be. EEwwwwww, how gross.'

'I will need to do some tests on it, them, that. Just leave it with me. Come back tomorrow and I will let you know more then. I also want the other vets to have a look at it, if that is all right by you?'

'Yes, no problem. Only too happy to get some kind of help. That poor Hedgehog with that growth. Yes, see what you can do for the poor chappy, then.'

The vet smiled and ushered the woman out of the room. She left Jeff and Hedgy in the container and quickly ran into the opposite room.

'Ginge, come and have a look at what I've got.'

'What, I'm extremely busy.'

'Please Ginge, I desperately need your opinion about it and right this minute.'

She was with a patient and growled, 'sorry, I need to see my colleague. I will be back in two jiffs.'

The boy with his rabbit said, 'that's all right. We'll wait.'

Poppy, the vet went to show Ginge her astonishing animal but found that the Tupperware had been knocked over onto the floor and the contents gone. Panic struck everyone.

Poppy shouted, 'where's it gone?'

Ginge angrily retorted, 'I don't know you were supposed to be looking after it.'

The Vets ran into reception and Ginge asked the staff, 'have you seen a Hedgehog with a penis on the top of its body?'

All three receptionists shouted, 'What?'

Poppy butted in, 'whattttt, your avin a laugh.'

Ginge replied most indignantly, 'no I am not. If you'd have come quicker, you would have seen it for yourself.'

Poppy replied, 'a penis on a Hedgehog? You really have lost the plot, Ginge.'

'Dam you. Let's just find the bloody thing. I'm going outside to see if it's lobbed itself down the street.'

'Yes, and I am going back to my patient to help a real creature in distress, thank you.'

The whole reception area was full of pets and people, giggling at what the vet had come out with. Ginge was so embarrassed. She crept back into her room after walking in without Jeff and Hedgy. Fully dismayed, Ginge wanted to hide underneath the carpet, any carpet so that nobody could see her.

DISTRESSED, DISTRAUGHT AND DOWN RIGHT DIZZY

Hedgy's legs ran like a wheel. They legged it to the nearest, out of site garden. A bush with heavy foliage was their only hidden comfort. Hedgy, with belly flat out and legs stretched to exhaustion lay just catching his breath until his breathing became agreeable to his mouth. Jeff was the same but he was just in sympathy with Hedgy. Hedgy looked up after a few minutes and said, 'what you panting for. I did all the running.'

'I did all the worrying and all the thinking. It takes a lot out of you, this brain work you know.'

'Yeah right. Thinking, huh. You couldn't think yourself out of a wet paper bag. In fact you'd get stuck.'

'Oh Yee of little faith. I got us here didn't I?'

'As a matter of fact, no. My legs, body and intuition got us here, Mr Jeff, know all.'

'Well lip service my knob. You have no idea.'

Hedgy said, 'the coast is clear.'

With that, he dashed across the road and onto another garden where there was undergrowth and plenty of distress free cover, for now anyway.

Jeff mumbled, 'one scrape after another. When is it all going to end?'

'What, what did you say. When's it going to end? I'll tell you when it's going end, when you get off my back and run off. That's when.'

'I have told you for the fifty fifth time, I can't. I am well and truly stuck to you, so get used to it.'

'Easy for you to say. You're not the mug doing the bloody ferreting legwork. I am.'

A foot plunged deep into the soil in front of them. A little boy stopped and tried to find his football.

'Nigel, where did ya kick it? Was it in ere? Oh, it's all right. I got it.'

With that, he kicked it back into play.

'Phewwwwwwwwww, that was close. Another inch and me bloody nose would have been stood on.'

'Hedgy, find us somewhere safe, for god sake.'

'Bloody god has nothing to do with safe. There's nowhere on this god's planet safe. Get real.'

'Just bloody move, will you?'

Hedgy legged it further down to a block of flats. He was absolutely exhausted and dropped to the ground, which incidentally, was not very far. He sat for ages listening to Jeff going on about how they would be caught, somebody would see them, it is not safe here, and it is dangerous to just crash as you like. Eventually with fifty minutes of nagging, Hedgy decided to climb the steps to the flats and headed for a safe place. He saw a silver little room, cosy, comfortable, and looked good for their needs. He carefully lifted his tiny legs over some grids in the flooring and quietly made himself comfortable in one of the corners. Jeff thought, I have been in one of these before but where? A metal door with huge gory graffiti words and drawings shut in front of them. Their eyes just fixated, horror set in and they sat there frozen like the game of statues. Once the door closed, it went silent. The feeling of claustrophobia crept in and a smell of dust mixed with anxiety filled the space. Nothing happened. Still nothing. Suddenly, the floor jumped and boomed at the same time. Their bodies bounced to the motion, up and down, and then a grinding motion with a distinct panic of floating without moving whooshed their whole beings. The lift was now travelling but their stomachs were not. It was awful. The shear experience of none compliant bodies wanting to go another way apart from the lift way, was very sickening. The ripple effect started to become regular and the sensation balanced. The lift suddenly just stopped them in their tracks and they bounced all over again. This went on for roughly three more times, then people entered and left the room. The next time Hedgy got ready to leg it. He was seriously feeling woozy. The lift bounced its last bounce and Hedgy jumped and bounced out of the door when it opened. Solid ground at last, he thought. He kept walking fast until he could see a safe, dark area for them to disappear into. They stood there waiting for something else to happen. Their bodies were petrified for something else to reach out and catch them.

A woman came out of one of the block of flat doors, noticed them in the corner, picked them up, and carried them into her home.

'What you doing, put me down?'

Jeff growled, 'stop squeezing my bell end. You're hurting me. Stop it. Hedgy, tell her?'

She hurried into her kitchen, found a carrier bag, and put them inside it. Then she put them on the table. Hedgy looked up at Jeff and asked if he was all right. Jeff did not answer as he was listening to a conversation between a man and a woman in the room.

The man said, in a Black Country accent (West Midlands), 'what the hell are yow teckin?'

The woman replied, 'It's an oliday and I is teckin every fin.'

'If yow fink I am gunna shut that Keas, yow got anuver fink cumin.'

'Down't be stupid, it's a light weight.'

'Yeah, just like yow, a light head more like.'

'Down't be cheeky. Just pewt this in and clowse the ruddy thing, then.'

She passed the man Jeff and Hedgy in the carrier bag, but as he did so, they fell out into a glass of ouzo the woman was drinking. It was full strength and bloody potent. Jeff tried to gasp for breath but only got alcohol. He gulped the lot down and eventually cleared the bottom of the glass. This was neat stuff and very strong.

'What yow drinkin? That's me practice run fer me olidays.'

The man quickly picked up the bag without looking what was in it and stuffed it into a tiny, squashed space in the suitcase. Luckily, for the both of them, he had left a little air pocket for them to stay alive, hopefully.

'I feel funnoy. That stuff's strung. I'm gewin dizzy.'

Hedgy replied, 'you're not the only one.'

With that, they both passed out in a drunken stupor.

CRAVELLING CHE HIGH LIFE, YEA, HA!

Daylight made their eyes squint. The suitcase had been opened.

'Brad, ave yow sin me new sunglasses, you know me spectacles that ave reactor lights in um?'

'Yow need to find em, cos yer as blind as a bat wi out um.'

'I know that's why I'm asking yow, cretin.'

'I'm goin down tut beach. Are yow cumin?'

'Not wi out me damn glasses I ain't, no.'

'Fer blasted shite gob woman, there stuck on yer ed.'

She glared in dismay and replied, 'silly me.'

'Cum on then, suppin time.'

'What d'ya mean, suppin time. Yow said down tut beach?'

'Yes woman, you swim, I sup.'

With that, they both took towels, costumes, the woman's handbag, his wallet, suntan lotion, plus Jeff and Hedgy in their new home, the carrier bag.

The journey swung with a vengeance. Jeff was just about to throw up on top of Hedgy, when he screeched, 'you dare. You just bloody well dare.'

Jeff swallowed quickly and gulped it down. He felt he was going to throw up again just as quickly. He thought this was disgusting to say the least. He was turning green with liquid and carrots and peas and worms and grass and, oh god. He squirted his colourful mouthful all over Hedgy, the floor, in the carrier bag and all over his balls. The putrid smell was liquifiedsick.

The woman dropped her bags at the side of one of the sun beds, sat down, and called one of the waiters over. He came immediately with a smile and a wanting to serve her.

'Hello madam, how can I be of assistance?'

'Ooh assistance, hey.'

She chuckled with the waiter and ordered some ouzo. This was the traditional drink of Greece and made on the island of Crete. The locals make their own special mix and sold it to tourists, such as the woman in question.

'Eeeeeww, what's that smell.'

'It's not me.'

'It's around here somewhere.'

He detected the bag and saw the array of sick colours dripping from the contents. Luckily for Jeff and Hedgy, they sneaked out just in time and glided gently into a pool of water at the side of the pool gardens. The gardens had been hosed down and pockets of pools of water were scattered. Hedgy was so relieved to find a washroom at his feet and scratched and cleaned, cleaned and scratched every last bit of gunk off his body, feet, and hands. Unfortunately for him, when Jeff washed higher up, all the debris washed its way back down to Hedgy and he had to wash and scratch, scratch and wash all over again.

The ground was very dry even though it had just been watered. Tufts of grass grew in patches and there was not much ground cover. Hedgy spotted a half-eaten burger and chomped to his heart's content. Jeff was still feeling sick after the effects of the alcohol and wretched a few times, but nothing happened. Luckily, for Hedgy, he was able to fulfil his stomach hunger with his burger.

 A baby girl was waddling by and noticed Jeff. She grabbed hold of him and took them for a walk along the swimming pools edge. She decided to take them for a baby swimming pool wash and flung Hedgy in feet first. Then she decided to drown the both of them. She lifted them out just in time and made a splash with Hedgy's body and feet. She loved her new toy and thought it funny to splash everybody she saw in the pool with it. Hedgy passed out, went limp and Jeff felt paralysed from the balls down. He stood erect for the shear horror of his flexibility to become more of a weapon if he loosened up a bit. Eventually she was fed up with her new toy and flung it in the branch of a bush nearby. Hedgy woke up an hour later to realise their predicament. Jeff just slumped over for comfort and relaxed for the first time since he was attached to Hedgy.

'If we just stay here we should be safe.'

'How D'you work that one out?'

'Well, firstly, we are above the ground, nextly, we are a good distance from the ground and mostly because nobody can see us, cos I can't see anybody.'

'Ummmm, I'll go along with that. Just keep still. Stop wriggling.'

'My nose can smell delicious BBQ yummy, yummies, and it's coming from over there.'

'Look you had a burger earlier and I'm not into BBQ's, so stay put and don't move. Savvy?'

'Savvy.'

The night was warm and the atmosphere entertaining with holidaymakers enjoying an evening listening and dancing around the pool area, chomping on culinary delights. Each smell wafted up Hedgy's nostrils and bloated his gastric stomach to heaven. He was hungry, so hungry. His teeth chewed the evening breeze and tasted every aroma. His nose wiggled until it could waggle no more.

Jeff could not eat directly, nor taste anything. His sniffing sensitivity was off the menu. He literally lived off the culinary education of Hedgy, which was dodgy, very dodgy. Hedgy had a tendency to eat anything going, good or bad and just for the hell of it. They both eventually fell asleep until the early hours of the morning, when they were showered with a powerful spray of water for the gardens pleasure. Hedgy held on to his branch as if it were his life. Jeff twisted his shaft around the twig to help hold on. After about an hour, the gardener stopped his daily watering and put his hose away. The sun was warm and the day was fresh and young. Hedgy spotted some BBQ droplets that the gardener failed to clean up. He immediately let go of the branch and clambered down to ground level. Jeff tried to hold on but his shear weight made him follow Hedgy. Jeff also thought Hedgy was not exactly lightweight himself.

Sneakily they reached the smell of heaven. Hedgy tucked in as if there were no tomorrows. Jeff just sat there waiting for the nourishment to reach his body. All those additives, colouring, fat and all that E Coli. A stray cat clawed at Hedgy and screeched. Its teeth glisteningly white and scarily pointed. Its whiskers stuck out of its face like spikes and its whole attitude was ready to fight to the death for what was left of the daily takings of food. Jeff and Hedgy slowly withdrew their whole beings and said, 'nice pussy, you can have all of it. Nice pussy.'

Then they ran hell for leather down the track to a wooded area. The trees were sparse and the ground jagged with boulders, bricks and wooded debris. Hedgy clambered for miles until they reached a couple of Jetties on a rock side. Jeff looked to see what was in the vessels moored up and toppled over into the small ferryboat. Crash, bang, and wallop they went. Bruised and battered they arranged themselves out of sight. A couple of mini buses arrived on shore and the tourists were helped onto the ferryboat.

'Is this the ferry to SPINALONGA ISLAND?'

'Yes lady dis is.'

She clasped the hand of the man she was talking to and climbed down to one of the empty seats. Jeff and Hedgy were underneath her.

Jeff said to Hedgy, 'what the hell is SPINALONGA thingy place, then?'

'I don't bloody know. Never heard of it.'

All the seats were taken and the ferryboat left for the island in question. It took roughly an hour to get there. Hedgy's leg was caught in the woman's handbag strap as she carried it off onto the island. Hedgy wriggled free but in the fall damaged one of his legs. Hedgy hobbled to safety under some huge boulders and then dragged himself up the entrance steps, round the corner to one of the derelict houses on the island for safety. Out of sight was out of mind, he thought.

'God, that hurts.'

'Why, what you done?'

'I landed funny when we dropped from that bloody woman's handbag. Bitch could have held on a touch more.'

'Look drag us over there and you can rest up.'

'Bloody drag, it bloody feckin hurts.'

'Just get us out of sight and you can rest up all you want. I can see people coming towards us, and if I can see them, they can see me. Just bloody move you're torso, now, go, go.'

Hedgy moved them, still in pain and dragging his bad leg into a ditch not far from a house with four doorways. Both could fit into the crevice made for them. They heard tourists with a local lecturer up above their new temporary accommodation. The lecturer told the history of the island. Spinalonga Island is called by the locals, ISLAND OF TEARS. Where it was cut off from the mainland because it was meant to be a safe haven for lepers.

'This was an incurable disease and even today they do not know its origin.'

The lecturer went on to say, 'but they have found a cure for it. Therefore, nobody worry about getting the disease while you are here. Come on let's look at how they lived and the hospital that helped their terrible demise and lives.'

Hedgy was in a panic and shuffled out of the hole.

'Come on we're not stopping.'

'You can't get leprosy, he said so.'

'I know, I heard him too. Come on; let's get to one of those boat things.'

'You're frightened, actually scared of getting leprosy, aren't you?'

'No, just move your arse. Help me get to one of those Ferry thingies.'

'He said you can't bloody catch anything. Didn't you listen? Oh yeah, I forgot nob rot.'

'You could get your nob rotting of stinking flesh. You know the smell of the old Spinalonga.'

'Just shut up. I can't catch anything. He said so, didn't he?'

'Look, I'm balancing.'

'Yes, just balance better to the right so you don't put pressure on my bad leg.'

'Hedgy, I'm about to topple. Waaattccchh out.'

Too late Hedgy and Jeff gambolled down the hill and onto a huge flat rock. They landed sprawled out on what looked like an ancient slab. Tourists were walking in all directions and suddenly, Jeff became the centre of attention.

'Eewwwwww, look an old ancient phallic symbol.'

'What's a phallic symbol, Mommy?'

'Ooh, it's just an ornament of old. Your Dad's got one.'

Her father looked round and then looked at his wife as if to say she has passed the buck on explanations. I will just have to pass it back.

'Tabatha, D'you want to come with Daddy to some other buildings to see how the people lived back then?'

The woman put her husband's black Stetson on the top of Jeff and balanced him upright. She then sat by him and demanded that before they went off that they were to have a family group photo. A nearby tourist acknowledged what they were trying to do and volunteered to take the picture. The woman handed the tourist the camera and hey presto, the deed was done. Tabatha did not ask any more embarrassing questions, so onwards and upwards they marched.

They forgot their Stetson and Jeff could see nothing. Jeff deliberately pushed them off the slab after at least ten more snap shots were taken. Tourists thought it funny that a Stetson on a slab was history in the making on an historic island. The Stetson chin rope tangled around Hedgy's feet and felt quite comfortable for it to be able to stay there.

'Don't move. Just don't move a muscle.'

Jeff froze. Along came a slithery, winding snake. It was only a baby but it looked dangerous all the same. Hedgy gently turned his head and at the side were more of the critters. Mommy snake was sliding towards them in a rage. They had fallen into a family snake pit. Nobody moved a solitary muscle. Their ergonomics balanced precisely. As quick as they came, as quick as they meandered off down the rough, rugged, rocks.

Jeff collapsed in relief but the hat was still hiding his prowess. Hedgy too. For a moment, Hedgy had forgotten his pain and the swelling in his leg. They just stiffly stood waiting for something else to happen but after ten or so minutes it was silence, calm, and eventually a relaxed state of mind. The hat came in handy because the heat sweltered around them but the Stetson kept the sun's rays from penetrating their bodies. It also made a safe-ish haven for them to hide.

AT LAST HE IS A PHALLIC GOD

The hot sun lowered its beautiful warmth and spread slowly into the Cretan Sea. The colours glowed for miles and rippled with the waters playful whispers. Jeff wallowed in the indulgence of peace, harmony, and calm. Hedgy snored his head off and played in his ocean of dreams, twitching frequently. This only disturbed Jeff occasionally. He ended up laughing at the funny shape Hedgy made with his nose when he was just about to twitch.

Later, in the evening moon, you could see glimpses of caretakers to the island roaming around and checking for people who were lost and tourists wanting to spend the night for the hell of it on the island. Others wanting souvenirs of glass, rock, or trying to pinch historic stones or items found. They were also just managing their business. So many tourists per day walked around the island. It was their job to make sure everyone on the island was safe. Any movement, they would know about it. Jeff and Hedgy felt a little safe but always had feelings of being found and careful not to alert any being, animal or human.

It was a night to remember, so peaceful. Both had regenerated and woke up feeling a new day was upon them. Jeff asked if they could go to higher ground because the tourists would be on their way shortly and he did not want to be noticed.

'Hey, move, some Ferryboats are coming. Tourists have just arrived and ready to step out to greet us.'

'Ok, ok, I'm moving, I'm moving.'

'Up there, it's out of any bodies' way.'

'You try clambering up there with a gammy leg and a moron on your back to boot.'

'I am not a moron.'

'Hey, dam, watch where you're going.'

'Lean with me. Not against me. Dick for brains.'

'Woke up with a sore foot and a hangover still, have we?'

'No actually, woke up with a moronic Dick still stuck to me back and giving stupid orders to boot, actually.'

'Oh aren't we tetchy today. Just hurry up. Look we're nearly there.'

'Where?'

'There, that ledge there. Yes, you've got it. You're not as decrepit as you look, are you Hedgy?'

'Was all right till you pounced on me. Cheeky bastard.'

'Now, now, mind your language. You shouldn't swear in front of your younger's.'

'Get away, younger's. You're much older than I am. You've got wrinkles on your tinkles and spots for eyes on your penis. Young? My arse is younger than you are. Give us a break.'

'I bloody will if you don't stop being horrid to me. Can't we at least be civil to each other?'

'Yes all right, you start first then.'

'Start what?'

'Being bloody civil.'

'I am trying to be. Shall we start again then?'

'If you bloody like but don't involve me. You make me so chuffing angry. Just shut up. That might work better.'

'Aha, we made it.'

Hedgy stretched the very souls of his feet and stood on all four stubbles of satisfaction. Jeff looked around and could see for miles. They were where the tourists could only admire. Jeff flicked off his Stetson and bared all.

Wrinkly or not he stood out like a humongous phallic symbol. As he admired his stance, he noticed some tourists looking and pointing at him. A French woman's eyes rolled with excitement at the size of Jeff and told the others of the phallic symbol she had caught a glimpse of. A small crowd appeared and in no time, Jeff was famous. He had been photographed from so many different angles. His popularity spread in a short space of time. For the next couple of days, Jeff was a film star. All the tourists had a picture of this penis, which was turned into a relic from Spinalonga Island.

Hedgy was wasting away and Jeff felt faint a few times. In the baking heat, they needed fluid and food to keep them going but there was not much on the Island, only bits of eaten sandwiches and seawater. It did not rain once. Earlier in the week, they managed to find a can of coke with an insect crawling out of it. They could not afford the luxury of which they shared their fluid with and so gladly supped with the best insects in town. Jeff put his hat on. The sun's heat was too hot. He flopped inside it and Hedgy sat with belly to the floor. That was where they stayed for the rest of the day, until night came with a cool breeze.

SUGAR AND SPICE AND ALL THINGS PRICKLY

Hedgy awoke after a good selection of snoring capabilities. Jeff, baggy eyed through lack of sleep, heard rustling down on the ground where they were spending the night.

'Hedgy,' Jeff whispered, 'what's that?'

Hedgy whispered in his terrified voice, 'I don't know.'

'It's coming from over there. No, there. No there.'

'Make up your bloody mind, then. Where?'

'There, no there, no over...'

'Arrh, it's one of me. Aarrrrhhh.'

'What, arrrhhhhh.'

Hedgy screamed, 'it's chasing us.'

'It's catching up too.'

The creature pinned them to the corner of two old building walls. Hedgy raised his front paws off the ground to defend himself. Jeff did not fight, as Hedgy squashed his huge body up against the brick wall. The moonlight was full on and Hedgy could see with squinted eyes, a mirror image of himself, almost. Hedgy after a few seconds, squashed upon the brickwork noticed that he was looking at a female hedgehog and nothing like him. Her hair was glistening in the moonlight. Her snout moist and tender and she had the strongest slender legs he had ever seen. It was love at first sniff. His eyes were a little crossed but he had fallen for this gorgeous wonder and nothing but his bounding heart was being used. His heart melted when she touched him. Suddenly, he became a puppy of love, sensual, lust loving, romantic fool. She stepped down, ruffled her coat of many thorns, and walked away as slowly and seductively as she could.

He laid there on his back against the wall, not understanding what had just happened, how fast it had been, an overwhelming gut ache, and wanting to see her again.

'Ok, it's gone. You can stop crushing my bollocks now.'

Hedgy's breathing was heavy and his thoughts were elsewhere's said, 'what.'

'Come on, we can't stay here all night. Anyways, what was that thing?'

'What, what thing?'

'Something bloody chased us. That thing. You know the ghost of the island. The terror of all terrors. That thing.'

Jeff did not see her go as his head was being squashed behind Hedgy.

'Ummm, yes she's gone now.'

'She's gone, who's she for god sake?'

Hedgy told Jeff to shut the hell up and went into the nearest building. Jeff did as he was told and fell into a much needed sleep. Hedgy could not sleep. He had met an angel of a female. Hedgy wanted her to have his babies.

Hunger for Hedgy was no problem because all he could drool about was his new found love. He thought about her all day, until night showed up again. The anticipation of seeing her made him positively ill. He had palpitations and heavy breathing when he heard the slightest rustle.

Out of the blue, with no sound apparent, she confronted them both. All she saw was Hedgy. She was curious as to his manliness and wondered did he have what it took to be her Hedgy. She began to squeal and Hedgy instantly without any thought for Jeff started to chase her. Hedgy was acting as if there was no Jeff and he was a free Hedgehog on the chase for a mate.

'Hold on, what's that noise.'

'What bloody noise. Keep quiet will you. This is a delicate situation I'm in. Just sit back, shut up, and enjoy the ride.'

'Well, whatever you say, but be gentle with me, ha, ha.'

'Quiet, you'll put her off.'

She started grunting, huffing, puffing, sneezing, and head butted Hedgy.

'Hold on lady, don't do that to my mate. Go and huff and puff at some other stupid fella.'

'For god sake, Jeff, shut the hell up. She is supposed to do what she is doing. It's called being a Hedgehog, stupid.'

'Well, I never. What a stupid ritual and it's going on forever.'

'Look, she calls the shots, so shut the fuck up.'

Hedgy was beginning to feel tired and worn out from all the exertion she was making him do by running all over the Island, it seemed. Out of the blue, she gave into his sexual needs. She flattened herself on the ground and lowered her quills. She then, pushed her rump up for Hedgy to mate her. It did not take long and Jeff was definitely along for the ride that he never in a million years expected. Hedgy in love, who would have thought it. As quick as she came, she left. Hedgy was so happy, relieved and content with his masterful mount, progressive and proud that his love life had been fulfilled that night.

The next day the weather was very cloudy and cooler than usual. They stayed put in the house from whence they were chased and hid in a corner not far from where Hedgy was attacked by his beloved. Some tourists approached with a guide. He was explaining that the part they were in was originally the hospital where the lepers were treated. He went onto say that the people were sent to the Island for safety and to make sure that they lived in isolation away from anybody else, so that nobody could catch the disease. He went onto say as well that they have never found a cause for leprosy but they have found a cure.

'Well, we already knew that cos the other guide told us when we first arrived.'

'What was that?'

One of the tourists was startled and happy to point out that a hedgehog had crossed her path. She was also amazed at how quickly the hedgehog ran.

'It's her. It's thingy. It's the love of my life.'

He screeched for her attention but she was too frightened to answer. The tourists suddenly heard his call and looked around. The guide laughed and said, 'yes, we too have wild life and hedgehogs are nocturnal, so it shouldn't be out this time of day. However, did you know that our hedgehogs are sacred creatures of old?

Because they have been known to make love standing upright and their manner of mating is reminiscent of humans. Sometimes they mate face to face. In Greece and perhaps other countries, they are also a delicacy.'

Panic set in. Hedgy was in a terrible state.

'Jeff, I have got to find her. If they do, they will eat her.'

'He was talking in general terms, not about your lover. For god sake Hedgy, get a grip. You really have got it bad haven't you?'

'Afraid so Jeff. Come on let's get out of here. We got to find her before they do.'

The tourists could not quite see Hedgy and Jeff. They snook out under their feet and legged it down to where they heard her calling. They tiptoed past the balloon man but Jeff caught his shaft in the ropes of the balloons. Both were lifted sky high and chased with the wind behind them. Hedgy looked up and sure enough, he was well and truly wedged in and tangled tight.

'Wooowww, here we go again.'

'Hedgy screamed, Hellpppppp, helllllppp.'

He could see his new found love as she looked up at him. It was a helpless case of just fly and hope for a healthy landing. The other thought was, but where?

'Hang on Jeff. Don't you let go of anything, you hear'.

'Look I'm not just hanging around for my health, you know. It's wrapped tightly. Just enjoy the view, and what a view.'

'We're getting higher and its getting bloody cold up here.'

'Wiggle your legs Hedgy, and get used to it. I think we're going to be up here for some time.'

They heard a terrific bang and saw a bird drop before them.

'Dam, that one got shot. It must have been too near the bloody balloons.'

'Christ, D'you think it got shot at with an airgun or did the bloody balloon just pop?'

'I don't know I can't see over the mass of colours from here.'

'Well its dead, stunned or blasted unconscious, cos it passed me like a lead balloon.'

'We're lowering. Maybe the wind has dropped or one less balloon means one less balloon to keep us up. Or you're too bloody heavy.'

'I've got to have a crap. Ha, ha, suddenly I feel like a bird. Can you see any cars from here to drop me shite on?'

'Ha, ha, ha.'

'Go on then, just do it. It should make us very much lighter. You've always been full of shit. Go on, do it then?'

Hedgy blew his cheeks and put all his pressure of force to one end of his body and his bottom exploded with what felt like buck shot from a sawn off shot gun. Pellets fell in rage and ripped through the wind in force.

'Hang on Hedgy. It's my turn next, ha, ha, ha.'

'You dare, you just bloody dare.'

'Oh dear, too late. Aha, just kidding, aha.'

'Honestly, some people. You're a gas a minute, you are.'

They had flown through pockets of air for hours and the sky was beginning to go grey, cloudy, and quite dull.

'D'you think it's going to rain, Jeff?'

'Uhh yes. Too late here it comes.'

'Dam that heavy water. It feels worse up here and colder. It's just a combination of weathers with no integration of barriers. It won't rain for long, it never does here.'

'How the bloody hell D'you know?'

'Just an educated guess, I guess.'

'Well guess again cos it's getting worse.'

'Stop bloody moaning. It'll be over before you can say; Hedgy is an irritating arsehole of a bollock of a mate and needs pissing on. Oooooopppppps, too late.'

'You heathen, you pissed on me. You bloody shite master. You actually pissed on me.'

'Look it's warmer than heavy rain. Anyway, you should be grateful. The piss will make you feel better and a lot warmer.'

'Like fuck. I owe you one, you Cretinous, crap, cunt, wank, dick shite, bastard.'

'Oh, come on don't talk like that. I thought you were my friend.'

'Yeah, like fuck. My best feckin enemy more like. Fuck off.'

'And where do you expect me to fuck off to, Hedgy? Heaven maybe? I'm not ready yet.'

'They wouldn't have you anyway. The pearly gates would be full of crap and the only way you're going to get through them is climb but your too dam lazy for that. And, if you climb them the caretaker would punch you in the face and tell you that's from Hedgy, ha, ha, ha.'

'Now come on Hedgy be nice to me. I'm holding the rope, remember.'

'Now Jeff, don't do anything silly. You know I was only joking.'

'Well, say sorry then.'

'What me, say sorry to you? Like fuck, I will. You pissed on me you, you arse wipe.'

'Go on, just a little apology. I will forgive you instantly.'

'Fuck off, let go. No, I mean it let bloody go. I can swim for it.'

'Yes, back stroke. I've already experienced your swimming abilities.'

'Just a wittle sorry to Jeff?'

'Fuck off. Wanker. I hate every wrinkle in your god dam body. I hope the rope strangles your gonads.'

Jeff started to wriggle and pulled at the rope as if to release it.

'No Jeff, no, please no. I don't want to die. I'm too young for all this.'

'All right, just say the magic word then.'

Hedgy mumbled but Jeff could not hear.

'What', as he shook the rope again and again.'

'Sorry you wanker.'

'Now that's better Hedgy.'

'You do realise this is abuse and when we land you are in for it, don't you.'

'Look, there's land ahead.'

'Where?'

'There, on your right.'

'Can you make the balloons go a little more to the right so we fly over the bloody land instead of around it?'

'I'm trying, I'm trying.'

Jeff wriggled like mad to get the balloons to go more to the right. They hit another air pocket and dipped roughly fifteen feet. Their stomachs felt left behind and the tickle inside was a strange kind of nice. With this drop, they noticed the wind change and made them head for land and possibly a landing.

ITALIANO, FERRARI, AND MAFIA.

Relief and revenge was in the mind of Hedgy. He suddenly thought his leg did not ache as much as it did. Perhaps it was getting better. He also thought, let them hope the landing would be easier on him this time, and to be aware of how to land, hopefully, better than last time.

Land was now underneath them. The fork of Italy had arrived and now the rope that Jeff was attached to started to slip from around him. He flopped in half to get a better grip.

'Hold on,' Hedgy screamed,' I don't want to die. I'm too young and it's a hell of a drop from here.'

Jeff could not speak and he twisted his whole being around that rope. He held on knowing his life depended on it. It started to rain again. This time it became apparent that this made the rope very slippery. Hedgy could see land all around now and said, 'we've got to get lower. We are far too high.'

Jeff tried wriggling again but the rope slipped completely. Jeff rolly pollied over Hedgy. They both fell like a ton of bricks, simply full weight down into oblivion. Their lives passed before them and Hedgy's psychological state was out of order and mentally read, not in.

Duff, they both landed. They sprung up like being on a trampoline into the back seat of a brand spanking new red shiny Ferrari. They bounced quite comfortably on Jeff's shaft.

They landed just in time because the roof was automatically closing, as they laid there bewildered. 'Arrivederci, Marcello.' ('See you later, Marcello')

'Who's that?'

'Sounds like, ummmm Italian.'

'D'you think we landed in, ummmm, Italy somewhere then?'

'Well, we've got a good chance, but where?'

'Are you all right Hedgy? How's your leg? Did you land all right? Are you hurt in any way?'

'What's the niceness all of a sudden? If I remember, you pissed on my head and now you're asking if I'm all right?'

'Look, I've grown attached to you. What's your problem?'

'My problem is being attached to you. And for the record, I'm allllll right thanks.'

'That's good then. Nice to know.'

Hedgy sniffed and could smell herbs and he could not quite put his snout on the other aromas around him.

The door of the Ferrari opened and two men got in the front seats. They looked to be in a hurry and fiddled about with a huge bunch of keys. After fumbling for about ten minutes, the engine roared, and the driver, drove as if he was being chased. Hedgy could still sense food around but could not find it.

'Aha, Veloce (quick), go, go, go.'

'Mettere il piede al metallo. Abbiamo disogno di raggingere Lisbona, Portogallo in tre goirni.' ('Put your foot to the metal. We need to reach Lisbon, Potugal in three days.')

'Stiamo ottenendo spese pagato per quest? L'ultima volt ache era una fregatura.' (Are we getting paid expenses for this one? Last time it was a rip off.)

'They're talking funny Jeff?'

'Sounds, ummm Italian and I think that's where we dropped into?'

'Bloody foreigners. I can smell lovely, delicious, ummmmm yes, pizza. Anchovies, tomatoes, oregano, bread fresh and luscious, gorgeous mozzarella. It's oozing my name. Can't you hear it? It's saying eat me I'm yours.'

'Hedgy, shut up. I'm trying to listen to what they are on about.'

'I didn't know you spoke Italiano.'

'I don't, but they've said something about Lisbon, Portugal and something else with three in it. I can't quite figure it out.'

The man on the passenger side threw a box toward the back seat. Jeff saw it hurtle their way and leaned enough for them to fall to the floor of the car. They landed on the pizza.

'Oh Jeff, thank you, thank you. I will forgive you everything, even pissing on me from a great height, thank you.'

'Ok, ok, just shut up and eat then.'

Hedgy munched his way through three quarters of a pizza and Jeff fell asleep. When he awoke, the car was still in motion and the outside lights had gone out. Hedgy was snoring, so Jeff gave him a nudge. Hedgy grunted in anger but did not break his dreams. His snoring stopped and he settled into a purring sound. The men did not notice his noises because they had the radio on. Jeff could hear 'leavin on a jet plane, I don't know if I'll be back again,' and hummed to it.

For the first time since Jeff and Hedgy stuck together, this time was spent doing absolutely nothing. Jeff looked up to the occasional light in a town they passed through or from other vehicles going past. He was now getting a little bored and wanted some action but, nothing. They spent literally hours in the back of the car.

Jeff saw blue lights and the men were panicking.

'Più veloce, più veloce, la polizia dietro di noi. Corsia laterale veloce. No, corsia centrale.'('Faster, faster, police behind us. Quick side lane. No, middle lane.')

'Abbiamo bisogno di mantenere la calma e rallentare in modo da non sospetta nulla, quindi zitto.'('We need to keep calm and slow so they will not suspect anything, so shut the fuck up.')

The police sped past and did not even notice their car. Jeff wondered why they would be worried about the police. Were they criminals that had escaped form a prison or perhaps axe murderers, or even gangsters stealing cars? All Jeff could do was entertain his thoughts as to why?

After a while, the men calmed down and drove quite sensibly. It made sense to drive normally and not to draw attention to themselves if they were avoiding the police for some reason. Blue flashing lights and sirens came from nowhere. A police officer drove his vehicle full speed alongside the Ferrari. He pointed to the man in their car to pull over. The man stuck his middle finger in the air and ripped down the motorway in the central reservation at high speed. Another police car pulled alongside the right of the Ferrari and waved for the man to pull over. The man swerved and with his foot fully down on the accelerator tore away from the police chase. By coincidence, another red Ferrari was ahead and the driver of the fleeing car caught up with it. He mimed a challenge to the other driver and coaxed him into a Ferrari special speed bonanza.

Side by side and with growling engines roaring together, vrooooooomed down the busy motorway. The police sirens flickered in the distance. They had no chance. Once the race was on and the speed was full flow the man sped up an exit road and flew away from the crime and getting away. The police from the other side of the entrance to the motorway told the other police cars to follow the other Ferrari and not theirs. The man driving slowed his Ferrari right down and disappeared through the winding, local avenues of Italy's famous small and narrow roads. Five minutes had passed. No police cars, no sirens, just a steady flow of a few cars passing each other.

The car stood out like a sore thumb. Italy is renowned for its sexy, masculine, purring machinery.

'Wow Hedgy, we are sitting in a Ferrari that was built in Modena, Italy and owned by Fiat.'

'How D'you know so much, then?'

'I don't, I just do.'

'You don't make sense. You either do or don't.'

'Oh stop asking stupid questions. You're awake then.'

'Oh, oh yes well, just.'

'I was getting bored on my own.'

'I got gut ache. Need a dump.'

'What again?'

'I had one ages ago.'

'Yes, a little birdie told me.'

'Arh, very good, Jeff.'

The car stopped abruptly and a gang of men surrounded the car.

'Mi è stato detto, Gregon è stata presa in consegna da noi.'('I was told Gregon was taking over from us.')

A man in a silver grey, shiny suit strolled over and replied,' E allora? ('What of it?')

Both men got out of the car and gave the keys to the suited man. The man looked back in the car and noticed his box on the back seat. He re-opened the door, grabbed the box, and stood by his partner.

'Wheres il nostro viaggio di ritorno, quindi?' ('Where's our return trip, then?')

A stocky, powerfully built man pointed to a warehouse and said, 'La cosa gialla, laggiù. ('The yellow thing, over there.')

Che il giallo Fiat, laggiù.' ('That yellow Fiat, over there.')

The gang were sniggering.

'Non scherziamo. Ci torneremo in un vettore Banana?' ('You must be joking. We're going back in a Banana carrier?')

The gang still laughing gave them the keys and they walked off to their new destiny. The Ferrari was looked over outside, very carefully and glimpsed at on the inside. That was such a relief for Jeff and Hedgy.

After about three and a half hours of just waiting, they heard the car rev up and driven into a cargo trailer. Then, the light went out as they closed them from the outside in.

'I don't think we're going to get out of here alive, Hedgy.'

'Jeff, I'm scared.'

'Well, you should be.'

'There's something else in here with us. I can hear it.'

'Now I'm scared. What is it?'

'How the hell am I supposed to know. Anyways, you're the brave one. You get out and see if you can find out.'

'Not bloody likely. I'm staying put.'

'Well, shut up then and stop being horrid.'

'Me horrid, me horrid. You've got the wrong guy, pal.'

'There it goes again. We're moving. We're being lifted.'

'Arrrhh, that noise. Was the chain to attach this bulky box to lift it onto the great big ship that we are going to sail on, to god knows where?'

'A ship? You never said anything about getting on a ship.'

'I didn't know dummy.'

'How are we going to get out of this, then?'

'I think we should go back to sleep because we are going along for the ride, Hedgy.'

'I'm scared, Jeff.'

'Just close your eyes and think of, what's her name. Oh I forgot, you didn't ask did you.'

'Shut the fuck up. Don't you ever talk about her again, got it?'

Hedgy shook himself into a comfortable spot, and then shook himself again, just to let Jeff know that he was in charge.

They slept for hours and hours. It did not feel as if the ship moved at all. It must have been the huge size of the thing. It was bigger than the largest whale and as massive as some Islands they had visited or saw. When they woke up, they were bored because there was nothing to do but listen to strange creaking, bangs and a very loud silence. Neither of them could see anything either. Their voyage was forced none exertion. It was days before they finally got some action. They felt the ship move differently and stop. The chains were finally heard and the clanking got louder.

'We're being lifted, Jeff.'

'Yes, I can feel.'

'They might drop us.'

'Yes, I know.'

'Into the water.'

'Don't be bloody stupid, we're on a tremendously large vessel. We would be dropped back into it first. Come on use your brain.'

'I am. We could be dropped after being lifted out of the ship and transported onto land, nearly.'

'You really take the piss. You know that?'

'I'm scared. I want to get out now.'

'Just stop panicking. Look, as soon as we get out of this hellhole, we'll find something to eat. Now concentrate on that thought for now, Hedgy.'

A boom, thud, and shake as it hit the ground from being lowered. Then the cargo container was attached to a lorry base and their box of tricks was driven to a segregated area of the docks. Both of them were ready to escape at the first glimpse of daylight. No daylight and not a glimpse of any way out. Two more days, at least passed.

'You promised me food.'

'I promised you nothing. I took your mind off being scared by suggesting food. It worked didn't it?'

'No it bloody didn't. Now I'm starving. My stomach thinks my throats been cut and my tongue feels like sand paper.'

'Look, if it's any consolation, I am just the same.'

'Well actually, no it's not.'

'Have some card board.'

'What?'

'From the pizza you ate. Maybe it might have a touch of flavour in it. After all it is Italian.'

'You eat feckin card board. You got no chance, and ruin my guts? No thanks.'

'After all you've eaten already; your guts are well and truly used to rubbish. Ha, ha, ha, ha.'

At last, daylight, fresh air, (well air anyways) and movement. Jeff and Hedgy had no plan of escape and squashed their bodies under the driver's seat. Hedgy could still smell pizza from the cardboard and thought that Jeff was right. That cardboard was beginning to smell very yummy, yummy and inviting to Hedgy's taste buds; especially being too close with his nose that was pushed firmly onto the cardboard box.

A gang of men arrived to look the car over. Some Italians spoke in broken English and others in American slang. They agreed to move the car and Jeff over heard one of them say something about the Mafia and the ganglands of America. Two men got in the back of the car. One man noticed the pizza cardboard container, picked it up, and threw it out of the window of the car. Gregon sat in the driver's seat and his co-pilot was an American, dressed in American baseball attire. He could hardly sit in the seat because of his huge body mass of muscle.

'Cccoookk, we exchange at a warehouse at Miami.'

'Yeah, you got that right.'

One of the men that were squashing Jeff and Hedgy to the metal of the seat was actually standing on Hedgy's tail. He was not hurting him but Hedgy could feel it all the same.

'Jeff, give me some room, will you?'

'There is no room with his clod hoppers in the way.'

'Just a fraction. I want my tail back.'

'I'll try but I would not say I could do anything.'

Jeff did exactly what Hedgy wanted and his tail was moved from under the gangster's foot. Hedgy, at last could rest a little easier now.

It was not far to the Warehouse and was abnormally huge. It was made of steel girders surrounded with corrugated strips of four- foot by nine-foot wide steel sheets. The light grey made it look even larger inside. It also looked to be a brand spanking new build. Gregon ripped into the dust as he drove the Ferrari into the building. He parked it majestically in the middle as the other gangsters were waiting in anticipation for their arrival. Street sweepers, colt Pythons, knives, sawn-off shotguns browning automatics, and specialist equipment was pointing at the Ferrari as Gregon stepped out of the car. The two men sitting at the back were ready with Beretta's and Benelli's. One even had a Mauro Battaglia. Another car pulled into the warehouse but this time it had attached to it a machine gun coming out of the roof. It was a big motherfucker with adaptors all over it for security. One man jumped out of the vehicle with body armour on and on full alert bounded toward the Ferrari.

Gregon said in an authoritative voice, 'show me the colour of your money, and you can have the merchandise.'

Gregon made a hand gesture to one of his men to stand by him. He was also playing macho man and with his stance looked to be important.

There was a man heavily dressed in a highly expensive business suit and a long coat over his shoulders. He had a matchstick in his mouth and was chewing the ends of it. He shouted as he walked towards Gregon.

'I have a problem. I have not enough cash but I do have plenty of drugs you can sell. More than enough for this transaction and possibly we could do other business as well. I provide and you sell for me.'

'No deal.'

'Why, I have more than enough in merchandise for the exchange.'

'It's too, umm, how you say, dodgy. Der risk is no good.'

A man from the other car parked at the back strolled over to Gregon and whispered, 'we can do this. We have connections. Barter for more merchandise and we will have a deal.'

'Ok, dis is how it is going to be. You give me double de amount of merchandise. We sell it, if it makes us money. If we get no trouble, then and only then will you get der Ferrari. If we get trouble you get nothing.'

'Noooo my friend, no.'

'Dat's the offer, take it, or leave it.'

'All right, but what do we get?'

'You my friend get a long wait.'

The businessman went to walk away and get into his car. His men followed. Gregon's men and the heavy machinery car boxed them in. Gregon went over to the businessman and said, 'hand over what little cash you have. That suitcase will do and open the boot for the merchandise. The men in the businessman's car went to get out but Gregon's men stuck their foot and body weight on each door. The businessman had no choice. He was in no position to argue. Gregon cleared him out. He put the money suitcase on his car and said pleasingly, 'aha, that's what I like to see, all the money is here. Can't you count? We will take the drugs for your lies and deceit.'

Another four by four drove through the dust and when it settled a little, the Americans started shooting at the heavily machined vehicle. Gregon's men dispersed behind the cars but one or two of them were shot. They managed to get into the car. The businessman's car stood still because somebody had shot into it and the car would not start. As quick as the four by four arrived, just as quickly it left the warehouse. It returned a few seconds later but this time coming from the other end. More shooting. A couple of bullet holes ripped into the paintwork of the Ferrari. Gregon was able to grab all he had found in the businessman's car and managed to get into the Ferrari.

It all went quiet. A shuffle and a scrape were heard behind the American car. A head of a Feg pistol (fegyver es PJK-9HP) popped up and fired at the tyres of the Ferrari but missed. Ping sounds were heard as the bullets missed and hit concrete. One of Gregon's men got out of the car, crawled on the floor by the side of the Ferrari with his M1911A1, and shot at the American car. At the same time, another American gangster jumped up to fire but shot at his little finger. He began to squeal, rolling around where his body dropped and screamed in excruciating agony. Jeff heard somebody say loudly, 'ha, yeah, one down just a few pussy cats to go.'

Hedgy heard a shuffling commotion by their side of the car. He blinked and glared, then noticed two guys side by side with one giving the other instruction as to where to go next. One went left and the other sat up, hiding behind one of the wide pillars that were holding up the warehouse and behind some boxes. They both got into position and waited. A deathly silence of anticipation had spread in every nook and cranny of the warehouse.

There was whispering in Italian that could be heard but not deciphered. More shuffling. Again, a deathly silence that lasted a whole minute but felt like forever. Shots from all directions came out of nowhere. As quick as they popped up like metal ducks and targets in a fare ground, as quick as they disappeared again. The in-depth, tense atmosphere spread like a bad smell and infected every one's anxiousness. Then more shuffling movement in all directions could be heard and the dust from the floor made parts of the warehouse difficult to see. Another car drove, skidding into the parked American car. It stopped centimetres apart and the people in it were shot at from the opposition as they did so. Next all hell let loose. Bodies dropped like apples from a tree. Dumf, hitting the deck as death claimed the movement of life from their last breath. Others were spitting blood and their pain had cried for all to hear.

Jeff noticed the Italian that hid by the boxes, was sitting in a pool of blood. His accomplice struggled to get to him and assessed his situation.

'Dove ti ha colpito?'('Where are you hit?')

'Ooowe, al mio fianco.' ('Ooowe, my side.')

'Dove, non riesco a vedere, troppo sangue?' ('Where, I can't see too much blood?')

'Sshhh, tranquillo. Saranno sentirti. Con le mie costole. '('Sshhh, quiet. They will hear you. By my ribs.')

'Metti le mani fuori. Userò la mia cintura per cercare di fermare l'emorragia.' ('Put your hands out. I will use my belt to try and stop the bleeding.')

'Va bene, leggermente più alto, superiore a quello.'('All right, higher it slightly, higher than that.')

'Cosa, dove, lì?' ('What, where, there?')

'Oowwwe, sì, ci.' ('Oowwwe, yes there.')

'Sssshhh.' ('Sssshhh.')

The make shift tourniquet was put on to stop any more blood loss, but his clothes, body, floor and himself was still dripping. It looked like the squeezing of the tourniquet nearly worked.

'Resta lì. Cercherò e si arriva in ospedale '. ('Stay there. I will try and get you to hospital.')

'Ok'. ('Ok.')

'Non passare su di me adesso, vuoi?' ('Don't pass out on me now, will you?')

'Noooo, ok, ma sbrigati.' ('Noooo, ok, just hurry up.')

'Gyga, non lasciarmi.' ('Gyga, don't leave me.')

'Tornerò prima di poter dire, figlio di puttana.' ('I will be back before you can say, mother fucker.')

Gyga crept to the end of the packaging and then saw that the coast was clear. He made a hesitant dash for it. He reached the Ferrari and threw himself down by its side. Phew! He thought that was lucky. They must be dealing with their injured too.

Gregon was watching every move and asked in a whisper, 'Va bene, leggermente Più alto, superiore a quello.' ('What's up? Is Jabba dead?')

'Non ancora, ma sarà se non lo facciamo arrivare a un ospedale.' ('Not yet, but he will be if we don't get him to a hospital.')

'Quanto male è lui? Dove ha trovato un tiro? '('How bad is he? Where did he get shot?')

'Egli sanguinare a morte se noi non lo muoviamo, ora. La sua squadra sta svuotando tutto il posto '. ('He will bleed to death if we don't move him, now. His side is emptying all over the place.')

'Ok, ecco il piano. Si ottiene lui e portarlo qui. Poi lo prendiamo in ospedale '.

('Ok, here's the plan. You get him and bring him here. Then we take him to hospital.')

'Ok, ecco un altro piano. Si ottiene in macchina in fiamme, guidare a Jabba. Aiutiamo a prenderlo in macchina e poi portarlo in ospedale, in corsia di sorpasso '. ('Ok, here's another plan. You get into the flaming car, drive it to Jabba. We help get him into the car and then take him to hospital, in the fast lane.')

'Chi è incharge qui? Ora mi ascolti. Lo si fa a modo mio o niente '. ('Who's in charge here? Now you listen to me. You do it my way or not at all.')

'Se lo facciamo, che invaderanno il sangue e morire. Se gli diamo la quantità minima di movimento, allora avrà una possibilità di sopravvivenza. Così che cosa è di essere? '('If we do, he will flood blood and die. If we give him the least amount of movement, then he will have a chance of survival. So what's it to be?')

'Quello che ho detto, in primo luogo. Andiamo a prenderlo. Cosa stai aspettando? '('What I said in the first place. We go get him. What you waiting for?')

Gyga was flabbergasted and just stared in misbelief at Gregon. They both got into the car and the other gang members moved to hide behind the truck behind.

Gregon's car screeched into position and stopped as close as they could by Jabba.

Jeff had watched every move and ducked down when they became too close for comfort.

Gyga quickly sped out of the parked car and crouched down by Jabba.

His face had gone grey and clammy with the loss of so much blood and his speech slurry. Gyga asked him, 'Come va, Jabba?' ('how you doing, Jabba?')

Jabba holding his dripping rib cage said, 'Non mi sento molto bene. Sentire male. '('Don't feel very well. Feel sick.')

Nessun problema, abbiamo COMT a prendere in ospedale.' ('No worries, we've come to take you to hospital.')

'OOOOwe,   aaaarrrrhhhhhhhh.'   ('OOOOwe, aaaarrrrhhhhhhhh.')

'Bisogna stare un po', il mio amico. '('You have to stand a little, my friend.')

Gregon came around the other side of Jabba and demanded he get up. Jabba did exactly that. Gyga and Gregon got him into the car as quickly and as carefully as they could. The dirty dust violently swirled as they sped with Gregon driving. You could tell with Gregon's tenacity that he loved speed, danger, and being in control.

The fight was on again as they escaped. Shots from all angles and from a variety of guns went off. Gangland was still at work on both sides but it was time to go. Both sides were dying and they wanted to die another day.

DRUGS, MONEY AND THE KU KLUX KLAN

Gregon drove into a drive in. They had not eaten since yesterday and were very hungry. The food on the ship was not much to be desired. They got out of the car and Gregon put the sunroof down because the car was hot and stuffy. Gregon and his men went into the restaurant and sat down. Jeff thought out of sight out of mind and quickly got his thoughts together to leg it. Hedgy's left leg had cramp and every time he moved, the pain and stiffness gnawed at his eagerness to stay put, only until the cramp went, but no, Jeff decided it was now or never.

'Come on, move your body, quickly. Get up on that seat. I will help you.'

'No, I can't.'

'Now Hedgy, we need to move quickly. Now, just go will you?'

'I can't, it's too painful.'

'Every bloody time we need to move, you gabble on about pain or hurt or just plain old can't.'

'Move, pain or no pain. I ain't stopping in this red thing any longer.'

Hedgy lifted his good leg onto the raised bit in the middle of the car seats and prized himself up onto the seat above. Jeff bent his body around the seat, once up and rippled his fore skin into pushing them further up and onto the car's leather interior. Hedgy laid there with his cramped leg in the air and relaxed for breath. Jeff flung himself into a gambol and they flew out of the car and landed onto a paper bag. It did not break their fall and only made them query where they had landed. As quick as Hedgy's cramp came, it went. Hedgy found his new challenge and legged it to the nearest grassland. It was the only place he knew to have a chance of safety. A car pulled in and nearly squashed them to their death. Luckily, Hedgy with his newly found strength, moved sideways so as not to be made into hedgehog pate. The long grass covered their tracks, just in case anybody was following them but nobody even noticed them gone. Hedgy saw his favourite food, burgers, buns, French fries, and mayo. He sniffed for food, ate one or two, and moved on. He did not care whether anybody could see him or not at this point. He was starving, as starving as someone who got a degree in the school of starvingness. He just grazed all night and into the morning. In the early hours of the morning, he explained to Jeff that he had stomach-ache and could not move. Eventually, he emptied his bowels and felt a whole lot better, in fact ready to eat all over again.

'Hedgy, stop eating. We need a plan to move on. Any ideas?'

'Well, chomp, should we, chomp, crunch, where, chomp, ok, you tell me then, slurp, chomp, crunch.'

Jeff shouted, 'Will you stop eating and give me your full attention.'

'Uuummm, chomp, chomp, burp, burp, fart.'

'Come on just follow me.'

An American bus pulled up and Hedgy ran for it. He missed it because of his huge gut that was hanging on the floor, almost.

'Right you need to move this excessive weight gain, so walk.'

'What?'

'Bloody walk. Get going and don't stop till I tell you.'

'No, I bloody won't.'

Jeff started to deliberately shake his shaft from side to side. Then forwards and backwards.

'What you doing. Stop it.'

'Well if you bloody well won't move I will have to make you.'

Jeff carried on his wobbling until he could gyrate no more.

'Come on, just stop and I will walk, ok?'

'All right. Promise?'

'Bloody promise.'

Hedgy decided to succumb and to force his gait forward. It was not easy as his weight was humungous. As distance became measurable, so too did the stretching for Hedgy. Eventually after a mile or two, Hedgy felt normal. Jeff on the other hand kept falling asleep. With the occasional wobble, Jeff managed to stay on Hedgy's back, reasonably straight.

A young boy spotted them and ran over to pick them up. Jeff dodged him and Hedgy squealed, clicked, and popped as he ran across the road to try to get away from him. The boy followed. He had the hood of the Ku Klux Klan in his hand, managed to catch up to them both, and covered them with it. Luckily, for Jeff, the eyes were measured for him to be able to look through. Jeff and Hedgy played statues. They never moved a muscle as the boy uncovered them to find out what exactly he had found. He was pleased with his find and took it home. He lived in Florida, Jacksonville to be precise. His mansion was well equipped with fancy living. His bedroom was the size of a small shopping Mall and the toys he had would take him at least a year to play with. This boy wanted something different, dirty and rough, so he picked on (yes you have guessed it) Jeff and Hedgy.

Jeff and Hedgy stood on the boy's dressing table looking like an old relic, dug up from the back garden. His mother came into the room and asked, 'Ooooooooh, what's that Joe?' It smells of garbage. D'you want me to throw it out?'

'No Mom. I found it, it's mine.'

'Ok darlin but you got plenny of toys, why this monstrosity?'

'Found it, I like it, and it's mine. Just leave the hell alone, Mommy.'

'Ok dear.'

With that she walked out, defeated.'

Hedgy chuckled and whispered, 'Jeff, I think you look good in your new hoody.'

Jeff whispered back, 'shut the fuck up, and watch this demon child.'

The boy picked up Jeff with his Ku Klux Klan hood on and put them on the floor with some other toys that were covered in the same white cotton hoods with eyes cut out for the toys convenience. The little boy picked another couple of toys for victims. One was a cowboy, the other a large sheep and another was a strange looking fish. He placed them on top of some sticks he had collected earlier and placed the sheep in his newly formed bonfire. He then set fire to it. He started chanting, 'you will burn in hell for your sins. You are horrible and need to be taught a lesson. You are the enemy and we are here to serve.'

He repeated this over and over again. He also walked around the toys with Hedgy and Jeff on the floor. It was getting quite frighteningly hot and so Hedgy decided to gently prize them away from the flames. The flames were getting higher and the smoke was spreading. The boys Mom flew into the room. She was full of rage and shouted at the little boy to put the fire out.

'Get out of this room. You stupid child. Run, go tell your father to help. Quickly, now.'

The boy said, 'but, but it's my game. I am the Ku Klux Klan and they need to be punished.'

She then began shouting, 'Marvin, git your ass up here right now.'

'What the hell? Joe, go down stairs, now, quickly.'

The flames had enlarged so much and the smoke thickened.

'Marvin, just call the fire brigade, we can't control this.'

Marvin rushed downstairs and did exactly that. Within minutes, the flashing lights were seen and the fire engine was parked outside their house. Jeff and Hedgy coughed their way to the front door and escaped, but only just. Jeff had also lost his white Ku Klux Klan hood.

Jeff and Hedgy were free again. Free to choose their destiny and exhausted with their overwhelming ordeal. They sat for a moment underneath the fire engine, just to catch their breath, literally. After a while the coughing stopped and Jeff said, 'Well, what a bloody palaver. If it's not one thing it's another.'

'Yes, I know Jeff. Where to now? We can't stay under here all day.'

'Your guess is as good as mine. You choose. Our destiny is now in your hands. Just get us out of here.'

Hedgy went to step into the road so that they could get to the other side but a vehicle missed them by inches. Hedgy stepped quickly out of the way and veered off onto the path on the same side as they were already.

A stray dog confronted them and carried them off. He trotted for miles until he eventually ended up in a dilapidated, run down derelict, unsafe building. This to him was home. He balanced from one box to a corrugated sheet to more rubbish until he eventually came to his kingdom of peace, quiet and safeness.

He dropped Jeff and Hedgy in a small cardboard box, presumably to eat for his supper. Four tiny puppies, no older than a few days old lay down with their Mom and suckled from her. After lunch, the puppies played and one by one, she carried them to another box and placed them in again one by one for their safety. She ran off and left everyone to their own devices.

'We need to get out of here. I can see us becoming lunch.'

'Yeah, me too.'

Jeff pushed and fell on the side of the box it toppled easily and they balanced on everything they could to get out of there. They heard voices. American men. Sounded like a gang of them. Hedgy crept towards the entrance of where the men were and crawled inside the building. They could see mounds of white bags, piled high.

'Oh no, they're coming over here, hide.'

'I just heard him say.'

'This is Cocaine. It looks to be where they make it and store it.'

'D'you think they sell it from here as well, then?'

'Nah, I think this is the manufacturing place and they dabble in retail else where's.'

'There's so much of it. In fact, millions of dosh for the taking.'

'Hide, they're coming over here, again.'

Jeff and Hedgy wedged themselves into gaps between the packages. The men used a forklift truck to carry the bundles of Cocaine to a huge van. In the process, they also collected Jeff and Hedgy. Jeff and Hedgy could hardly breath, they were so squashed and confined.

Another journey to another place in another squashed up vehicle. They were getting fed up with their lot.

It was over an hour before the vehicle stopped. A familiar voice was heard.

'Gregon, vuoi che io a controllare la merce?'('Gregon,do you want me to check the merchandise?')

'Basta scegliere uno da sotto e assaggiarlo.'('Just pick one from underneath and taste it.')

'Bene'.('All right.')

'Troverete i nostri prodotti in buon ordine. Questo è il vero McCoy, genuina, pura come la neve in Alaska, e chiara come l'acqua di sorgente di montagna Valley in Arkansas '.('You will find our products in good order. This is the real McCoy, genuine, pure as the snow in Alaska, and clear as the mountain Valley spring water in Arkansas.')

'E' questo tutto? '('Is this all of it?')

'Sì'.('Yup.')

'Take it.'('Take it.')

'Basta ricordare, saremo voi a guardare tutta la strada, quindi non doppia croce noi o le vostre vite saranno annullati.'('Just remember, we will be watching you all the way, so do not double cross us or your lives will be forfeited.')

'Vieni Fella, fiducia in noi. Siamo dalla vostra parte '.('Come on fella, trust us. We're on your side.')

'Mi fido di nessuno. Soprattutto di Americano '.('I trust nobody. Especially Americano's.')

The American got the message, closed his mouth, and moved the merchandise into his vehicles.

'Adios, amigo's,' said the American man, and then drove off.

'The man in the driving seat growled, 'you stupid ass hole. You said good bye in Spanish.'

'Yeah, and?'

'They're Italian dope.'

'Oh, oh well, what the heck. Didn't like him anyways.'

In the changeover, Jeff and Hedgy were still wedged but not so tight. They could breathe easier, at least. Their journey was a long one and they had to lie in their own wee for hours. Hedgy, as usual, was hungry and his high sensitive nose went into override. He spent hours just sniffing the mid night aromas of good old American food places.

FULL OF EASTERN PROMISE

Travelling was laborious. Jeff and Hedgy just slept the whole way and did not even know where they were going. When the vehicle was eventually opened, daylight hit both their eyes and was blinded by the overpowering intensity. The heat instantly stuck in the back of their throats and the smell was a strange dry, herby aroma. Hedgy could not quite put his finger on the wafting scents of this strange land. They knew it was definitely somewhere they had never ventured before. Another lift into another place and more strange languages spoken.

The American got out of the vehicle, stretched his legs, and spoke to an oriental looking gentleman. He looked to have white pyjamas on with a bandage on his head. The strange personage also had on his feet, sandals. Not the kind of attire for heavy goods dispatching for working in (health and safety). Jeff thought everybody to their own, I suppose.

 Hedgy jumped and gambolled down from the vehicle and ran as fast as his legs could carry them both to a part built, made of make shift scaffolding made from thin tree trunks which was holding the ceiling up from the rooms. It looked to be open plan. It did not even have a roof. It also, looked very unstable. They heard screaming coming from the building, and saw some dark skinned men dashing towards them. A dark complexioned woman froze in one corner of the building. She had her knees up in front of her body and she was holding them with both of her arms. Jeff saw the gentleness in her eyes as well as tears. She was so scared of him. He felt helpless. He adored her innocence. He smiled at her and wanted to get to know her body better. He lusted to touch and caress her loveliness. She had long, slinky, shiny, black hair that reached to her bottom. Her face was a face of an angel, and her shapely, gorgeousness was slenderly sexy, and she glowed like a princess. Jeff simply lusted after her. He imagined all sorts of sexual moves that he could entertain her with. The power in him would make her wanting, needing and begging for more. His desire was making him sweat and drool. His overwhelming desire was to just to make love to her regardless of the consequences.

'Arrh, shag, lust, lust, lust, and more shag, lust, lust, lust. Wooowww, yes babe, no babe, might babe, would babe, no babe, nice babe. No, calm down I am becoming aroused. Oh, maybe not. I want a wee.'

Hedgy heard Jeff's weird noises and felt his uncontrollable palpitations, 'calm down, yes calm down. You will do us both mischiefs at this rate.'

Jeff's fantasy was out of control. As he looked, again he could see the voluptuous woman was leaving the building on all fours. She crawled to the entrance and managed to climb to her knees. She screamed again in horror, and then went out fast. Her arms outstretched, she screamed all the way down the street until somebody stopped her and asked her, 'what's the matter.'

About five Indian men came up to the house to try to find the horror within. Jeff and Hedgy legged it over the garden wall and landed into a crevice of under growth, rubbish, twigs, tree roots exposed, and an underground hole. They were safe for now, anyway.

Hedgy wondered, If he trod on a snail by accident, would that make me an animal hater, or/and would it mean I couldn't keep pets? Would that also make him a murderer? He could do time for that. They would lock him up and throw away the key, all because of not seeing a poor defenceless creature under his feet.

Hedgy frantically cried, 'get me out of here,' in his squeaky voice.'

Jeff replied, 'Life's given you an easy paper round, hasn't it Hedgy.'

'Arrh, I feel a joke coming on. Why did the monkey fall out of the tree?

'What, what are you going on about?'

'Cos it was dead.'

'That's not a good joke. In fact, it's stupid.'

Hedgy just wriggled his body with laughter.

'Another one. Are you ready for my master Joke, then?'

'Hell, no. Shut the fuck up. Oooh go on then. It better be better than that one.'

'Ok, here goes. If a man with a multi-personality disorder threatened to kill himself is it classed as a hostage situation?'

Yeah, got it so far. Carry on, then. Carry on, then.'

Ok, ok, ok. One cannot hold himself hostage it's just plain suicide.'

'Right, is that it? Hedgy, wake up. Is that it? Cos if it is its worserer than the first one.'

'No, listen. Get Steven to tell Jack to tell Steven that Jack said that Steven said Jack said to tell David that Jack said to Paul, leave it. Paul said why are you talking to yourself? But Steven said to leave a note for Jack that David's been here with Paul, cos Stevens out. His number in fear it being the wrong person.'

'La, la, la. I did not understand a word of it. No more jokes. I can't take your kind because they're stupid. Just like you.'

Both were just lying sideways and having weird thoughts, heart rate, palpitations and feeling nauseous. The effects of the cocaine were taking its toll.

'I feel fucked, me thinks.'

'I feel intensely cramped, me thinks.'

'Me feels sick,' as he vomits, 'oh too late. Me done vomiting, me thinks.'

Hedgy started to cry, 'I miss my girl, Jeff. I want to go back to Spinalonga. I need her, I want her, she loves me, and I know she does. Will she wait for me? Jeff, Jeff, Jeeffffffff, bloody answer me.'

Jeff was feeling dizzy, with a whole load of bodily heaviness and he was kicking involuntary with his head. He was also suffering with cold sweats and a runny nose.

'Jeff said, 'my body, I need a new one. This one is acting peculiar. I need sexual gratifications all over. Somebody help me please. He started to sing, an old Englebert Humperdinck Number called 'Please release me let me goooooo. I don't love you any moreeeeee.'

'Jeff, you in pain pal? My muscles and bones ache so much they're alien to me. Holy crap I've done it again. I got the liquid shits, Jeff. Yuk, it's all down my legs and in-between my toes. Jeff, its squelching, Jeff, Jeff, Jeffffffffff.'

'Shut the fuck up. Too much information, stop shouting and go die yourself quietly. I'm suffering here. I ache intensely and just want to sleep. I want to die quietly. Just let me go, Hedgy. Just let me go.'

Both of them were experiencing Cocaine withdrawal and found it immensely uncomfortable. The one thing they did not realise is Cocaine is highly addictive and severely dangerous, plus so easy to overdose on. Quantities of overdosing and killing yourself are very individual causes as each person's bodies are unique in tolerances. Neither could sleep and insomnia overshadowed their mood like a fog resting on a mountain. It lasted for hours. Both of them just agonised their very beings for, it seemed like quite a few days.

GHEIR GOING UNDERGROUND

Hedgy woke up eventually after trying to fall asleep forever. He had withdrawal symptoms of wanting to have more Cocaine. It made him feel brilliant to start but it had the effects of wanting more because of the drug making him wanting to be an addict. Jeff woke up a minute or two later and his body was severely ill with aching and wanting for more of the Cocaine. It was very addictive and the elements of happiness felt through the drug were captivating. Jeff sluggishly just sat on Hedgy. Hedgy sluggishly just felt total mentally drained, and both felt depressed. Their bodies did not want to function and their minds were blurred to say the least. Hedgy did not even give a shit that he fell asleep in his own poo. Liquid or not it smelt awful. The boys did not give a hoot and just gelled into a nothingness state of being totally off colour.

A whole in the ground appeared by the side of them. Jeff with half-hearted motivation stared at the darkness. The hole had a variety of tree roots down its cavity. Jeff and Hedgy just did not give a dam and sat heavily for a few more hours.

'Hedgy, you really do stink, pal.'

'Sorry, Jeff it was, I'm afraid, uncontrollable Diarrhoea and vomit. The vomit came later. Sorry.'

'What we going to do now then? We can't stay here.'

'Well, look at it this way, I ain't moving, nowhere, zilch, never.'

The daylight was fading and the shades of warm colours filled part of the sky. The reds were rich and the yellows blended to create the most unusual oranges, shaded with a background of light greyish blues.

Another couple of hours passed and their bodies, minds and aroma had not changed one iota. What did change their minds was a huge, fast moving, patrolling, Indian, humungous, native Rat. It had buckteeth and stared through the whole at them. It looked hungry and ready to pounce.

'Hedgy, runnnnnnnnn.'

The body moved but the mind ran out of the ditch and into the derelict building. Hedgy ran in circles and then back into the ditch. The rat followed.

Hedgy caught one of his feet in a collection of tree roots and slid down into the crevices of the deep winding slippery slopes ahead of them. They thudded themselves at the bottom and on a rock. Hedgy's belly was sore and bruised. They studied the area for anything animal, then vegetable and then mineral.

They were, somewhat safe for now. Jeff was still stiff with muscle spasms and Hedgy was still hung over. Both of them looked around to see if they could find a way out. Some dark patches in their new room had windows of darkness, painted with bits of red, orange, and yellow from the fading sky light, and filled with shadows creative of possibilities. Either way they were not pleased with their new accommodation.

In one of the dark windows the whole area moved slightly, Jeff thought. In the next window, another slow change of shift was apparent. Hedgy saw it that time.

'We are not alone, Hedgy.'

'Maybe just head for the light.'

'Sounds like a good idea.'

'Gently does it, don't wake the little critters.'

'Oooooooppps, too late. Just stay put Hedgy.'

An armour scaled head appeared out of nowhere, slowly and quietly. The creature looked to be sleeping and unaware of either of them. It was re-adjusting its bed and dozed off again. In the other window, the same happened but the other one's armoured scaly tail was huge. It also re-adjusting its tail wrapping so that it too could get comfortable. Only this time when the Pangolin adjusted itself it covered their escape doorway. Jeff and Hedgy were well and truly there for the night. It was just as well because neither of their brain cells were working to full capacity anyway.

The night came and closed all the light areas. The darkness scared them as the rustling and creepiness crept all around. They could hear what they thought was the Pangolin's moving and waking, ready for their search for food. After all, they were nocturnal and eager to eat. Other rustling, was unfamiliar and could not be understood where it was coming from. Perhaps the area of previous light. Jeff could see nothing but he suddenly heard a scurrying moving towards them.

'Hedgy run for the night sky on the left. Get us out of here. Go, go, go.'

Hedgy fell and heard shuffling. He picked himself up quickly and darted toward the night sky as Jeff had said. The moon was only half there and the shine was minimal. All the same, they could move into foliage and to another hidey hole. Both were alert for the rest of the night. Just before dawn, Jeff could see the Pangolins' coming back home to their resting place from whence Jeff and Hedgy intruded. Jeff could see a Pangolin browsing his home and tiredly gazed into Jeff's eyes.

With a deep-throated voice, the Pangolin settled his partner into her bedroom and slowly turned to his own. While he adjusted himself, he spoke.

'It is good of you to be our guests this night but I and my good lady need sleep. Please think of us as you talk very quietly and please do not bring anybody else into our domain.'

Jeff replied quietly and softly, 'we will try not to make a sound, and thanks for letting us stop.'

'You are most welcome. Now sleep.'

Next, they saw mongooses, lots of them. The family were merrily playing and teasing each other, oblivious to observers. Hedgy was surprised to see a beetle with such horns attached to its body. The stag beetle made its presence known just by walking majestically by.

Daylight crept into the hole and all was very, very quiet. The Pangolins had curled up into a comfortable window and fell fast asleep. There night-time munching had come to an end, until later. The Mongoose were happily skipping and playing close by and a King Cobra slithered into the hole. The Mongoose played with the King Cobra's tail like a toy, teasing and challenging its presence. The Cobra stretched its long body, lifted its majestic head, and spread out its facial cheeks. Its tongue protruded and played with the air scents all around. It hissed as a warning but the Mongoose was in a very playful mood. They tantalised and teased the space around it. The King Cobra hissed and darted in various directions. Its anger was apparent and its temper made known. It lashed out its jaw and teeth pushed forward to bite its prey but the Mongoose were faster and skipped around the Cobra ground in defiance. The King Cobra manoeuvred its body in such a way as to distract the Mongoose and made a quick getaway. The Mongoose are renowned for killing King Cobra's, so this one was lucky or very experienced in handling these creatures.

Jeff and Hedgy just looked and learned about the nature of Indian life. The entertainment was breath taking, weird and quite an education for both of them. They also felt not like doing anything for that day, just sitting and watching the world go by.

Jeff thought of life before all this and could not remember anything familiar. Little snippets occasionally jolted a tiny incident of his past but nothing significant. Hedgy could only think of Spinalonga Island and the love he had left behind. He thought of what could have been, how things could have turned out so differently if they had not been flown away like they did, and so many what if's.

JUST CRUISING

In all, Jeff and Hedgy relaxed for three days before thinking about moving on. They relished in the wild life and Hedgy kept them nourished with worms of the season, and dicey vegetation. Water was only a luxury in that kind of climate and so they found it in the plant life.

'Jeff, we need to move on. It's too good here and we are getting lazy.'

'I know but where to next?'

The locals started excavating the hole and shovels pushed the soil. Every living thing rushed out to get away for their lives. Hedgy was no different. They bolted to, exited, and fell down an embankment. The Pangolin's followed behind and rolled over Jeff and Hedgy in the process. The mongoose spread far and wide but met up later as a family again. On their arrival, Jeff and Hedgy were trying to figure a way out of there. One of the Mongooses decided to tease Hedgy, just as they teased the King Cobra. Jeff was in no mood. Another Mongoose came around the back of Jeff and pushed him by force on his shaft. Jeff was getting agitated and said, 'hey, stop that. Buzz off.'

A smaller mongoose crept up behind Hedgy and tried to pull one of his legs. Jeff felt the agitation and decided to act. He swung back and forth which gave him a swinging movement and smacked one in the gob with his tip. Then he flipped over to do a kung Fu kick and punched with his bell end another in their stomach. Jeff by this time was energetically angry and feeling ruthless. With the little one, he left that to Hedgy as he swung him around and pushed the little one into a prickly hedge. They were all winded but came back for more. This time Jeff was warming up and did his kung Fu fighting routine until all Mongooses ran off with defeat.

'Wow, where did that come from. I thought you were going to kill someone.'

'I was ready for death, trust me. And there's not mine. Come on don't run. Bring it on you cowards.'

'Remind me next time, not to get on the wrong side of you.'

'Right, what next. Shall we go find them and show them a good time for a change?'

'Uuuuuhhhhh, no. Just calm down and think. We need to get out of here. Have we got a plan?'

'Hell no, I want to fight. Come on, bring it on.'

'Jeff no, we gotta go.'

Jeff started to sway back and forth for more action. He was so wound up and did not want to wind down. He wanted to use the new found energy and hate he had cooped up. Hedgy felt useless against such force and just shut up. That left Jeff to have time to think and eventually he did, calm down.

Hedgy eventually started walking on the path below their demise. He slowly strolled, what seemed, for hours.

'Dogs, there's dogs. Look they're chasing us.'

'Runnnnnnnnn. Faster Hedgy, Faster.'

'I am. I am.'

'Get on that truck.'

'Where?'

'Over there.'

A ramp to the truck was running from truck to road floor. Hedgy lifted his front legs and climbed up onto the ramp. He managed to get them both up and to the front of the truck. The radio was blaring away in the front passenger compartment of the truck. The music that was playing was the beach boy's album. There was a rucksack and Hedgy and Jeff climbed inside it to hide.

After an hour or two the truck moved. The steering made the truck driver rickety. It clonked and broke sharply every time the driver stopped and started moving.

'What the hell.'

'My belly hurts with all that bumping and grinding. Somebody give it a rest, will you.'

Nobody heard the moans of Jeff and Hedgy.

The truck stopped and the back opened. A sideboard was pushed along the side of the truck and the driver carried on his quest. The bumping and grinding did not get any easier. The music changed to traditional Indian ballads. The truck was used for fetching and carrying various items of furniture, bags, rubbish, wood, and all sorts of moneymaking objects. Hedgy had sores all over his body from the friction caused by the motion of the truck. He needed to get off and as soon as they stopped, they got out and legged it all over again. This time they knew they were by the ocean because of the big ships moored at the docks.

'Pick one.'

'What D'you mean, pick one?'

'Look, just pick one.'

'All right, that one on the furthest bit by that posh ocean cruiser.'

'Right, I have changed my mind. Just get on that ocean Cruiser. We're going to have a little fun for a change. Trust me.'

'Trust you, I'd rather eat dirt with my bare hands and climb a slippery rope, rather than succumb to trusting you.'

'What's with the attitude? I thought we had got over all that nastiness.'

'Well, I haven't.'

Hedgy walked the plank to the deck of the ocean Cruiser. A rope was over the gangplank so as people would not come on board without permission. Hedgy sped under it and trotted along to an open door.

'Well, what an invite Hedgy. Somebody has left the door open for us. Don't mind if I do, Capitain.'

'Who you talking to Jeff?'

'Nobody Hedgy. Just having a little fun. You know that fun you know nothing about cos you are oblivious to it.'

'Sarcasm will get you nowhere, pal.'

'With you, I most certainly agree, pal.'

Both were all of a huff and nowhere to go. Jeff wanted to walk to the next door and Hedgy, just wanted to get out of trouble. He had had enough of escaping dilemmas. The pitter-patter of Hedgy's long nails tapped along the wooden decking. Even with a tiptoe, the sound was loud enough to be heard. Jeff said, 'come on let's find the dining room. It looks to be in this door, here.'

'If we go in there, we are sure to get caught and thrown to the sharks.'

'Look, gently does it. That's right just stretch a little more. Yeah, you got it.'

'Phew that was high.'

'Right head for the, ummmm, kitchen maybe or the buffet room. Over there look, it says all you can eat, Hedgy.'

Hedgy ran as fast as his legs could take him. At the buffet table, he jumped so high but could not reach anything.

'Dam Jeff, I can't reach. Find something for me to stand on will you?'

'Look, there's a chair, but you need to get something to get you onto the chair.'

'Dam Jeff, hurry up I need sustenance, nowwww.'

'Right got it. Stand on this ornament's hat and get onto the chair.'

'Right. No pushing. I want to do this myself.'

'All right, just hurry up, for god sake. I can hear voices.'

'Ok, ok, don't rush me. I'm on the chair and, and, and bloody and...?'

'Oh, you need to get down the chair because it's too far away from the food. Hang on.'

'I need to get down, don't I?'

'Uuummm, well yes. Just a sec.'

'Let's push the ruddy chair by the side of the ornament and just make sure the rest is by the table where the bloody food is, Dick for brains.'

'Ok SFB (shit for brains) move your arse over here so that our plan will work. Just hurry up. They're coming straight for us.'

Hedgy climbed on the ornaments hat, then onto the chair and onto the table. He scurried along the table and chose one or two items that he could feast on right away. His eyes and brain were working very hard to ascertain his next mouthful. Jeff on the other hand was having a panic because he was sticking out like a sore thumb and humans were nearly upon him. The cruise was a posh one. Everybody that Jeff saw was dressed for high society socialising. He saw the captain in the distance with his crisp white captain's suit and captains crisp white captain hat and his black shiny shoes. The tables around them were immaculately laid with napkins, knives, forks, plates, side plates and a variety of glassware from wine to water. All the condiments were squeaky clean and the whole room was impeccably clean and fresh. In fact, it looked like a nice new pristine ship. A couple spotted Jeff and looked down at Hedgy.

'Wow it's alive. Arrh, it looks to be a Hedgehog with some kind of cancerous growth on its back. Poor thing.'

The husband smiled at Hedgy and patted his spines, 'Arrh you poor thing. There, there, we'll help you but we have to get you out of here, else the captain would have you thrown into quarantine for the rest of our journey.'

'Ben, what you gonna do darling?'

'You get some lunch for us and find a romantic table for us. I will find a box and take this beaut down into our cabin until later.'

'Ok Hun, sounds fab. Talk to ya soon, babe.'

That was the plan and it was executed marvellously. Ben went back to the restaurant and he ate the food his wife had fetched for him. Both of them could not wait to get back to the cabin to see their new family member.

Grace, the wife had chosen a variety of food for Hedgy to munch on when they got back to their private quarters. She also put two tiny bowls in her handbag for the food and water ready to look after Hedgy.

When they got back to their cabin Hedgy and Jeff were fast asleep. As the door opened, Jeff and Hedgy were startled by the sound it made. Grace was so excited for her newfound pet, that she lifted them out of the box. Ben said gently, 'easy. Don't startle them.'

'Isn't it adorable? It's so cute. We will have to do something about that thing on its back though. We will take him to the vets, just as soon as we get home.'

'Is it a he or a she, Grace?'

'I honestly don't know. What shall we call it?'

'Well, if we don't know the sex of it, then it should be a neutral name, don't ya think?'

'Ok, we can call it, thing.'

'Well, that's not nice. How would you like to be called thing. How about a good old American name?'

'Like what?'

'Oooh now, let me think. How about Charlie?'

'That's good to go. It's a boys and girls name.'

'Charlie the Hedgehog it is then.'

'We shall have a guess what Charlie is, party.'

'Wowwww, yes, phone around and get some friends to have our very own cabin party. We don't want everyone to know we have a pet. They'll

All want one ha, ha, ha.'

Grace, while talking all that time was feeding Hedgy her food picking from the restaurant earlier and Hedgy was so delighted that he even licked her fingers clean when he had finished. With that in mind, Grace loved her newfound friend even more. Jeff ignored the relationship that was beginning to bond between Grace and Hedgy.

Next evening at roughly eight, some friends they had met on the cruise came to Grace and Ben's cabin party.

Mimmi and Oki were of mixed race match couple. Mimmi was from Hong Kong and Oki were from the Philippines but they spoke perfect English. Jasper and Pippa were both from Canada and their daughter, Princess was single and a very young twenty-seven year old.

Grace had arranged for a table to be brought in just for the occasion. Their cabin was in first class and the spacious surroundings made that quite clear. Everybody chose a seat and glared at the secretive cloth that was over something in the middle of the table. All were asked if they wanted something to drink first and nibbles were in bowls in various places set on the table. There was one bowl full of titbits for Hedgy. The guests did not know this though.

Oki asked, 'what's this cloth covering, Grace?'

Mimmi went to take some of Hedgy's nibbles and Grace said, 'don't touch those please, Mimmi. All will become apparent later. Here have these instead.'

Grace passed her another bowl of crunchy chip potatoes. All very Canadian as Grace, Princess and Ben were anyway. With everybody sitting Ben asked, 'is everyone comfortable?'

All said, 'yes thanks.'

'Then we shall begin. We are so excited.'

Pippa's eyes said it all. They stared widely on the cloth and sparkled with wanting to know.

Princess stood up and said beggingly, 'can I pull the cloth off now Par?'

'Oh all right then, if you must.'

The white cloth came off in a flash and revealed Jeff and Hedgy. Hedgy squealed and shoved his nose in the air ready to bite anyone who touched him or even came near his space. He also tried to curl up in a ball but all that happened were the spines on his sides stuck out and meant nothing for his prowess.

Pippa sat back and whispered, 'wow what a specimen.'

Jasper asked, 'where did you find him? What's that thing on its back?'

Oki just looked in disgust and explained it was a male deformed hedgehog that could be eaten. He also went on to say that in some countries it is a delicacy.

Grace found that horrifying that anybody would eat such a creature. She went on to say, 'well, this one is coming back with us. We are going to take it to our local vets, get it sorted and it will live in our garden with the others. We have about three, you know. They come and go as they please and we feed them every evening, just before we go to bed.'

Princess embarrassingly said, 'Pardon me for saying but that growth looks like a man's penis.'

Pippa sprang into laughter, 'what a penis, a man's dick for god sake?'

'Well hell, yes.'

Jasper replied, 'you could call it dick as its name then?'

Ben said, 'don't be so silly. Its name is Charlie, actually. We didn't know what sex it was, until you pointed it out to us.'

Princess argued, 'the more I look at it, the more I can see it's a man's dick, penis, taja, call it what you want. It's a dick.'

'And how many dicks have you seen in your lifetime Princess?'

'Well not as many as you Pippa, obviously.'

'Now, now, children. No squabbling. This is a cabin party not a truth game.'

Princess bitched, 'if it were, it would be full of lies and innuendoes.

Ben growled, 'now Princess, put your claws away. It's not that type of get together.'

Jeff and Hedgy were getting bored just standing around for their pleasure. Hedgy moved slightly to the right and back up again. All eyes were glued to their change of direction. The nibbles put out for them were administered to each guest. Grace moved forward in her chair and put the nibbles in front of Hedgy's nose. He sniffed it enthusiastically and took it aggressively with clicking and popping noises followed and then took them from Grace's delicate fingertips. Grace pulled back quickly with her startled glow of fear and excitement all at the same time. She then looked at the others as if she had just won first prize in a competition. Princess was next to feed Hedgy and he was a little more understanding of her intentions. He was also not going to bite the hand that was feeding him.

Oki decided to have a go. He stood up and leaned over the table. He dangled the nibble in front of Hedgy and decided to play by teasing Hedgy with it. Hedgy pulled up to bite the nibble but Oki pulled it away. Hedgy moved slightly forward and Oki put the nibble just far enough away so that Hedgy could not quite reach it. Hedgy was being agitated, started huffing, puffing, sneezing, clicking and popping to show his anger, and moved a little closer to Oki's side of the table. Grace said, 'don't tease him because he might bite you.'

Too late, as Oki was looking and listening to Grace, Hedgy bit what he thought was the nibble but he found himself in mid-air attached to Oki's finger. Now Hedgy had to hold on, otherwise he would fall and hurt both him and Jeff. Oki howled like a newborn baby. The whole ship must have heard his cry. The pain of Hedgy's bite ripped up his arm to all his emotional senses. Oki shook vigorously to detach Hedgy but Hedgy held fast. Ben came to his rescue and prized Hedgy's jaw apart so as not to hurt Hedgy but to assist in the withdrawal of his teeth carefully. It worked but Hedgy flipped and landed head over heels on Jeff's bell end. Hedgy, quickly got to his feet and legged it. At that precise moment, another guest arrived extremely late and as Beryl and Arnold opened the door to the cabin, Hedgy saw the land of opportunity and raced as fast as his little legs could carry him through it. Beryl looked and screamed at what she saw. Arnold saw and raced to catch them but Hedgy, surprisingly ran extremely fast.

Hedgy could only see a small corridor with lots of closed doors ahead of him. At the side of him was another corridor, so he raced down that one. Next, he saw an elegant carpeted stairwell and tried to climb it. Two hands came down on Hedgy, picked him up and they were put in somebodies black bag. Hedgy tried to wriggle, push, pull, and squeal but to no avail. They were rushed away to another cabin but this time it was not up top as they were but the person carried them a few stairs down.

'Jeff, we've been kidnapped and I can't bloody move from here.'

'Well, it looks as if we are going into somebodies cabin room. Squeal, Hedgy. One of the porters is coming and he might hear you.'

Hedgy made the most horrific, traumatic sound he had never done before and the porter questioningly asked the person, 'you all right?'

'Uuuummm yes, I just have a terrible cold you know.'

'I should go up to pharmacy and get something for that cough.'

'Uummmm, yes I will. Thanks.'

The more Hedgy wriggled the more the person squeezed them to try to stop anybody noticing the action packed bag she was carrying.

A door opened and Hedgy heard a voice say, 'Kali, what you doing back so early. I thought you were spending the night bingo-ing without me.

'Look, I have something to show you and don't scream. Hand over your mouth, now.'

Kali put her bag down on the bed and tipped it over so that the contents would fall out.

'Kelsi, don't touch a thing.'

Hedgy scurried to the edge of the bed and jumped off. Kelsi put her arms out almost instantly and caught them both.

'Now, now little fella, where D'you think you're going in such a hurry?'

Kelsi, still holding them gently looked down in wonder and caring as if to say, 'Arh you are so cute and cuddly.'

Kali smiled and stroked what little spines Hedgy had.

Kelsi said pitifully, 'D'you think he is going to die with that thing growing on him.

Hedgy replied but was never heard, 'he will certainly be the bloody death of me. Jeff what we going do now?'

'Isn't it the other way round. You have tried to get rid of me a number of times and you blame me for all this. It's bloody fate, that's what it is, just fate. Like it or not and it's no barrel of laughs for me either.'

'How the hell do we get out of this one?'

'We simply wait for the land of opportunity. It will come you just have to be patient. Something you're not good at.'

'I'm hungry. One nibble is not enough to sustain you and me.'

'Quiet, just wait. We will get food later. Just be nice to these creatures of want and need.'

Hedgy got used to being in the arms of a human of warmth and cosiness. He fell asleep in Kelsi's arms. Kelsi eventually fell asleep on the bed and Kali wrapped them all up in a throw blanket.

Next morning, Kelsi woke up stiff and forgot about Hedgy and Jeff in her arms. As she moved, they nearly rolled over onto the floor, but quick thinking Kali managed to grab Hedgy just in time and put all concerned back together again.

'They need a box or some kind or carrying case.'

'How the hell are we going to get through customs with them?'

'Well, I don't know. My plan has not got that far yet.'

'I know. Put it in the suitcase.'

'Nooo, he won't be able to breath. Oh, I don't know.'

'I know, put him in our toiletries bag with some metal stuff and he will not be detected, right?'

'Might work. Might not.'

'We've got to try something.'

'Yes but what? Look let's just put them in the suitcase for now and go get some breakfast.'

'Ok, sounds yummy.'

As she got off the bed with them both in her clenched hands, she carefully put them into the suitcase and zipped it up.

'He will be all right in there, won't he?'

'Yes, of course. We won't be long any way.'

As Kelsi lowered them in, she whispered to Hedgy, 'we will bring some breakfast back later. Now be good and don't make any noise, ok?'

Hedgy replied, 'yeah, like fuck we will. You piss off and we will find a way to escape, more like bitch.'

Kelsi heard nothing of Hedgy's reply and thought he was so cute, that it did not matter what he said. She loved him and felt sorry for his growth on his back, namely Jeff.'

A man on a loud speaker informed the passengers that they were approaching the Dominican Republic and that passengers could visit after they had docked first, in about an hour.

'Jeff, did you hear that. Docking in an hour. This is our chance pal. How do we get out of here?'

'Right Hedgy, move sideways quickly and I will lean and hopefully force this box to topple. Much like we did before.'

'Ok, Jeff.'

He ran and the box moved but not far enough. 'Hedgy try again, but from side to side this time and I will do the same.'

'Woo hooooo.'

The box fell over and landed with Jeff and Hedgy underneath it. The door opened and their newfound parents walked in chattering. They were so happy, relaxed, and wanting to get to know Hedgy allot better. Horror struck their faces when their eyes saw the horror of the box, moved. Kelsi immediately investigated underneath the box on the floor. As she prized the box up, Hedgy legged it out of the room and down the corridor. A very old lady saw him and screamed. Others that were in the corridor looked around to see what all the commotion was all about. Some saw Hedgy and screamed as well but others tried to catch him. Hedgy did an awful lot of ducking and diving until he turned a sharp left into a cupboard. Hedgy breathed as if he were having problems swallowing.

'They've gone. Just breathe normally. Try to breathe deeply. Slowly in and slowly, out. Try to...'

'Just.... Shut... the... fuck... uuuuuuuuuupp.'

CARIBBEAN FOR
SAFETY REASONS

Jeff and Hedgy had escaped luckily. When they gently and carefully opened the door to the cupboard, they found emptiness in the corridors and no sign of any interference. That was their role call. Quickly walking, Hedgy moved to a lift, which helped them get to the top floor. They very carefully looked around, ran for cover on the decking, and found it almost empty of people.

'I bet they've gone on the island to ravage all the shopping stuff and to catch up on all that is going on from the other passengers.'

'Yes, probably. I'm more concerned about getting out of here. Hedgy climb up there.'

Hedgy climbed onto what looked like a metal container. On the last step, he lost his balance and true to his immaculate form, fell. He landed on a soft-topped Jeep. A young woman in skimpy shorts and a very tight red T-shirt called out, 'anybody here for Cap Cana excursions?'

Some heads turned from where people were walking away to other ventures. Sitting in a pack were some people for the Cap Cana trip. The woman read out names as she was checking them into the Jeep. Grace and Ben sat in the Jeep. When it was full and everybody accounted for the adventure started with the representative talking about what will be happening with his or her fantastic experience. Hedgy, on the other hand held on as if his life depended on it.

The road was bumpy and the distance surprisingly short. The countryside was lush with foliage and an abundance of colour all around. The Jeep stopped and everyone got out. Hedgy let go of the canvas and laid belly down to recover from the trauma of jolting backwards and forwards. Not only that he tried to counter balance Jeff's movements too. All the same, they made it. The people left Jeff and Hedgy hiding and when the coast was clear they climbed down, and then fell the rest of the way to the dirt and boulders underneath their tread.

'Ok, we made it. Which way Jeff?'

'You choose this time. I got us into a mess last time.'

'Go on, we're used to a mess, and we're in it together, pal.'

'Oooooow, does that mean you love me Hedgy baby, gorgeous, cuddly Hedgy.'

'Jeff, don't push your luck Pal. Keep it clean. Honestly, you're off again. Get real. I am just trying to be nice for a change. Grow up.'

'Ok, ok calm down, get a life. I was trying to be friendly. Jumpy, jumpy. Do you know what left is?'

'Ummmm yes.'

He looked left with his protruding snout.

'Then, we will go right.'

'Very funny Jeff. D'you want to walk, pal?'

'No, I am quite comfortable right where I am, thanks. Go, go, go.'

Hedgy walked on to his right and trotted merrily along. Neither of them had a clue where they were going but their journey never did. All the countries they had already visited had never been recognised and no familiarity was apparent. They just took most of it in their stride and improvised.

Their journey started to take them inland of Montserrat in Dominican Republic. The humid climate wore both of them down eventually. Hedgy was thirsty more than hungry and could smell water at over fifty yards. He followed his nose and sure enough, water appeared out of nowhere. They came across a turquoise river of fresh, clean, clear, water. It gently trickled over boulders, foliage, and ooh a Mountain Chicken Frog.

'Hey, hi there.'

'Oh uh hi there, I'm Hedgy.'

'Hey, Hey, don't walk off. Talk to me.'

'Wat do ya wanta tark ta me fer?'

'Oh, you can talk to us then?'

'Yes, I is very cleva, ya know. I can tark to anyting but Umans, you know.' Dey don't listen and are stupid. Dey really don't understand me or mi weys.'

''How do you mean?'

'Well, com closer and I will tell ya mi story.'

Hedgy did as she asked. The creature sat with her fat belly on top of her bent knees. You could only see her toes sticking out from underneath her.

'Ok now, are ya sittin comfortably?'

'Of course we are. Just get on with it.'

'I can just go anytime ya know and I don't need ya mout shit. So my best edvice, is listen, don't interrupt mi and breed when I am finished. Got it?'

Hedgy said, 'Jeff shut the fuck up and stop breathing, will you?'

'I'm not, I'm not, I'm holding. I'm holding.'

'Then I will bigin. Once I ad a lover, not der best lover, granted but he was special to me. We ventured into der

111

Hotel room in town on der ground floor. We were lust lookin fer sumting to chew on. Somebody screamed der tongue off der feaces. Two female Umans ad never seen us befer. Security came, picked me mate up, and took im to der cook ouse. Dey boiled im alive.'

Hedgy could not believe his ears and said, 'Noooooooooo.'

'I ear dim squeal. It was der day part of mi died. I was carryin is children and needed im to fertilize me babies to feed and elp dem grow. It was never to be cos dey killed der Dadda. I eard leate dat cookin im der wey day did enhanced his flavour for Umans to chew. I can still ear der terror of is desperateness to survive in is pain cry. Nobody should ave to die like dat. NOBODY.,

'What happened after, then?'

'Well, I went back a mont leater to try and tell der Umans me story but dey just screamed at mi and threw me onto der grass gardens from der Hotel room. After dat me family were stopped from goin into der grounds and arll our food dat grew in der Hotel grounds was destroyed and leater, poison killed der rest of me family. Aunties, uncles, nephews, nieces, friends, and some enemies were just destroyed too. Der one's left moved ere where we are wid very little food and where Uman cars squash me family cos dey live too close to der dirt track. Dare is nowhere dat is seafe fer any of us. Umans, I ate dem. Dey destroy what dey don't understand and dey just don't ceare about anyting but demselves. Dey tink dey know us, dey tink dey souperia and know everyting. Dey are stupid. Dey know noting. Dey should live like der wey dey force us to live. In fear. We were appy to be left alone, ploddin along wid a great speace and place fer arl of us to survive respectfully. Life is ard enuf wid out Umans interfearances.'

'Tell her I'm human and I'll pass her message on.'

'I can ear ya. Yes, please,please,please pass it on befer it be too leate fer us to live.'

'Can I breathe now?'

'All reat, but only breed in yer own speace. Got it?'

'What space? There is no space.'

'Me point, exactly. Tell yer stupid Umans to give us our speace back as well.'

'We will, We will.'

'And anoder ting, Umans ave shagged everyting movin to become as orrible as they are.'

'Why do you say horrible?'

'Well, dey is careless, as in could not care less. Nasty der wey dey treat oder species and down reat nasty der wey day treat each oder. Umans are nasty to dem selves. Dis is a world to sheare not to teke over. It belongs to all of us equally and should be sheared accordingly. Dey ave not scraped der surface yet, of where Umans come from and of how to begin understandin anyting dat is not so called Umans. But when ya tink where Umans come from. Evolution is a bit of dis and a bit of dat. Umans are mongrels in der own history and a mixture of all moving and living tings. When dey gonna git it true der tick heads we is all connected, wedder we is likin it or not.'

Hedgy was in deep thought at what she had been telling him and remembered the time his father got run over by the road side at home. He stayed there for days and died in agony. His little brother was caught in a trap and they could not release his tiny body from the teeth of the monster that was set to kill anything that stepped in its way. His brother was just in the wrong place at the wrong time, just playing with his siblings''. It brought tears to Hedgy's eyes with all the people he missed so much, dead and alive. He thought of home but where was home. He did not have a clue where he was, let alone in the world and his predicament. The seriousness of his situation crept all over his body and he acknowledged that Jeff was to blame. He also kept quiet about how he was feeling because the adventures they had already been on and are experiencing were so different to his run of the mill life style. He was enjoying the not knowing, the horror, and excitement of their adventures together. Most of all he had found a friend that he could abuse verbally without malice. After his in-depth conversation with himself and gazes into his whole being, he decided enough was enough and it was time to move on.

'Well Froggy it's time for us to move on. Thanks for the lecture and hope you live a long and prosperous life but we have to go to new pastures green.'

'Well you is lookin in der wrong direction, cos der greenery you speak of is goin fast.'

'Come on Hedgy, that way.'

Jeff pointed to an opening in a wooded area that looked lawned and well kept. They needed food, water and a way out of the clutches of Mrs Mountain Chicken Frog. Neither of them noticed a wide stream running by their side and fell in. Luckily, for them it was not deep and the water carried on being clean and clear. Jeff could not see the bottom of the stream bed until Hedgy got his bearings and adjusted his stance for their walking swim.

Hedgy swam the shallows. His snout nearly curling to the sky.

'Not far now Hedgy. I can see land again.'

'You taking the urine, Jeff?'

'Yep. What a gorgeous day for a dip in a blue lagoon.'

'It's cold and very wet.'

'Uummmmmm strange, I never noticed.'

'Are you going to be sarcastic for the rest of the day or are you going to give it a rest, Jeff?'

Totally ignoring Hedgy, Jeff said, 'people, naked bathers. Wowwwwww, no clothes on.'

'Where? I can't see anything from down here.'

'Just swim, I'll do the looking, thank you.'

'I'm getting out now.'

'Oohhhhhhh, watch my bell end on those bloody prickly branches.'

'Oohhhhh sorry, forgot you were up there.'

'You did that on purpose.'

'Wow, look at the cock on that, it's huge.'

'What cock, where?'

'That gigantium over by the tennis courts. It's flopping around like no tomorrow.'

'Honestly, you've got a thing about cocks, haven't you?'

'No, just ones bigger and better than mine.'

'Why, is it a man thing, then?'

'No, it's, it's, a pride thing. To be stood out from a crowd thing.'

'Whattttt? You want to be noticed?'

'Of course, I am the best looking cock in the united Kingdom, at least. I could be the most orgasmic Penis in the whole world.'

'Arrrrh but then you saw these beasties.'

'Hide me quick. I don't want them to see my piece of dangling flesh.'

'I have heard that size isn't the question but rather how the bloody thing is used, isn't it?'

Jeff was so engrossed with hiding that he totally ignored again what Hedgy had said. Suddenly, Jeff went limp. His bell end met his bollocks and his foreskin had become a very thick collar. He could only see through his eyes if he squinted over his flaccid flesh.

'Oh Hedgy, what am I going to do? The competition is depressing for a midget like me. Take me away from all this.'

Hedgy just sat on the ground with his belly in warm grass, assessing their predicament, long and carefully. Hedgy looked both sides and noticed that Jeff had physically melted on top of him.

'I got an idea.'

'Whatttt, this better save me from death. Better still, shame.'

Before Jeff could say anymore, Hedgy was yet again, running through the bushes. He was trying to find some naked women to make Jeff feel more positive about himself. Unfortunately, Hedgy had found a mixed gender woman. She had huge breasts and a huge Penis. Her legs were well shaved and her face make-up was immaculate to match her black hair. She came over by Jeff and Hedgy, flopped her voluptuous breasticaters in front of Jeff and Hedgy, picked up the tennis ball, turned to face her opponent with legs apart, and dangled her swaying willy before them as she hit the ball.

'No, not a penis as good as that with a female's breasticaters. No please, no.'

Hedgy was feeling a crisis coming on and drove his body to move to more nakedness for Jeff. Jeff was still in a state of shock, negativity and his bollocks still wrapped in his skin. He peeped to see where Hedgy was taking him but could only feel the brushes of the plant life that slapped him occasionally as Hedgy clambered through. An opening appeared in front of them and to Jeff's amazement, gorgeous girls, young and older, curvaceous, slender, wispy, and simply fat women were soaking in the sun or like basking sharks in the clear waters of the Hotel pool. His bell end rose a little. His spectacular view enhanced into binocular vision, where they reached the deck chairs for their gatherings. Titillating conversations and girlie giggles were heard that echoed the walls of the Hotels poolside. The place was buzzing with voluptuous naked female powerful natural scents. Jeff had risen from his safety cloth and engrossed in the wonderful world of sexual want. He started to reek of sensual male, come, and get me, male hormones. His gaze danced faster than he could see.

Hedgy was relieved his friend had returned to heavenliness which he could manoeuvre more practically. Hedgy's problem was Jeff trying to look in all directions at the same time and still trying to balance the pair of them. Difficult, very difficult.

A middle-aged woman spotted the girth of Jeff, picked him up, and squashed them both into her beach bag.

'You bastard. Put me down, you old bat.'

'It's hot in here.'

'Nooo, where are all the titties, Fannies, and butts' wanted to see them all. Oohh please Satan get me out of here!'

Jeff tried to push and pull his way out with his bell end over the top of the opening of the beach bag but failed.

Hedgy, for the first time, since he did not know when, was NOT hungry. He was becoming accustomed to that way of life. He was just content to fall asleep, and thought he was finally getting used to change. This meant, grab all you can, when and where you can. Also, trying not to fall detrimentally and avoid hurting one's self in the fiasco. Oh, and lastly, look after each other. Hedgy thought as if he had a choice with Jeff the Maverick idiot.

Jeff stayed erect for his next encounter with the opposite sex venture.

'I've decided Hedgy; I am definitely, definitely a breast man.'

Hedgy snored with acknowledgement.

'I could also be a little bit of a leg man as well? Dam noooooo, I am a squidgy, arsy, bottom squeezing kind of bloke, Hedgy. Thank you for bringing me here. I needed to see some skirt less, skirt. You have cheered me up no end.'

Hedgy snored and rumbled again and Jeff thought it was an acknowledgement to what he had just said.

Jeff and Hedgy felt the bag lift and the woman's purse dug into Jeff's shaft.

'Heyyyyyyy Lady, watch what you're doing with that thing.'

Hedgy abruptly awoke from a wonderful dream with a grunt and a daze. It was about his beloved from Spinalonga Island in Crete. He was trying to get friendly and she danced a dance of the seven veils. They rubbed snouts, she ran away, she came back, it was a very long dream of repetitiveness, then he mounted her and then the bloody beach bag jolted him into a world of horrible reality. Hedgy squeaked in many rude words.

The woman, once in her Hotel room threw her bag on the bed. Jeff and Hedgy re-adjusted themselves once they hit the deck and crawled out of the top of the bag. She had a shower and as she came back into the room with a towel around her body, her husband opened the Hotel room door.

'Guten Abend wunderschön. Ich habe zu dir zurückkommen zu verwüsten.' ('Good evening gorgeous. I have come back to ravage you.')

'Du böser Junge. Sie sind zu früh. Ich wollte für einen Wechsel zum Abendessen zu kleiden. Wie war Ihre Golf-Expedition.' ('You naughty boy. You are too early. I wanted to dress for a change for dinner. How was your golfing expedition?')

'Ich bevorzuge die Sie ohne Handtuch und nackt auf dem Bett in eine verführerische Pose, mein Liebling sexy Hintern.' (I prefer you without the towel and naked on that bed in a seductive pose, my darling sexy bum.)

Das kann arrangiert werden. Lassen Sie mich nur die Befreiung von diesem Handtuch. Zwei Zecken.('That can be arranged. Just let me get rid of this towel. Two ticks.')

'Golf war eine Verschwendung von Zeit. Irgendein Idiot hat sich den Ball und es machte Zeb Nase bluten und möglicherweise gebrochen. Ich ließ ihn in ein Krankenhaus geht mit seinem Partner es empfohlen haben. Sie war eine miserable git. Alles, was sie tat, war zu meckern, wie er ihr Tennisspiel gestört.'

('Golf was a waste of time. Some idiot hit his ball and it made Zeb's nose bleed and possibly broken. I left him going to hospital with his partner to have it mended. She was a miserable git. All she did was moan about, how he disrupted her tennis game.')

'Klingt, als ob die Dinge nicht gehen, um für Sie planen, dann.' ('Sounds as if things did not go to plan for you, then.')

"Wir, ve hatte bessere Turniere." ('We,ve had better tournaments.')

'Komm her und macht mich stöhnen und jammern.' ('Come here and make me moan and groan.')

With that in mind, the husband quickly took his golfing attire and shoes off. Nakedness was not allowed on the golf course for safety reasons. To be quite honest, her husband was not a great fan of the naked flesh, exposed in public and was finding it embarrassing. It was also his first time at a naked naturist Hotel complex.

'Oi, oi, I was supposed to do that. Oi, oi, get in the bloody, feckin, bollockin, feckin, bastard, feckin, queue!'

Jeff saw her husband climb over her on the king sized bed. He took his time with a little foreplay. Jeff was fuming, he thought she picked Jeff because she fancied a bit of self-masturbation with a real live toy. However, oh no, she decided to use an automatic one instead.

Hedgy started laughing and his body chuckled too.

'Ha, ha,ha, you thought you'd get lucky, didn't you?'

Jeff turned and looked out of the window in disgust.

'What the hell am I supposed to do now? I am fully erect, willing and waiting, desperate for action and she pleasures herself on another prick.'

Hedgy still laughing, said, 'Pal, you've got no chance. You can't give her what she wants.'

'Oh and how D'you know. And what's that Pal?'

'Well, she needs a man that loves her and makes her feel cherished and loved, wanted and most of all, special.'

'I can do all that and show her lust, action, groping and so much fun. More than he can.'

Hedgy by this time, was rolling in a sideways fashion around the floor that they had just been pushed onto.

"Oh du schöner Mann, Sie. Gib mir mehr. "('Oh you beautiful man, you. Give me more.')

'Hedgy, you speak gobbledy gook, what they saying?'

Hedgy roared. In fact, his stomach was hurting so much as he rolled from side to side.

'Hedgy, stop laughing at me. Tell me what they said?'

'They said, mind your own ferreting business, and get your own room.'

'No they didn't. You're making it up.'

'Ha, ha, ha, how did you guess?'

They heard climaxing moans and groans, then nothing. Two sweaty naked bodies side by side. The heat in the room was already intense. Their work out, finished them off.

Jeff was borderline, depressive. He wanted to have a go but he was too far away from her. The woman had been pleasured and Jeff felt betrayed.

GOBBLEDY GOOK LAND

The woman treated Jeff and Hedgy like a plastic throw away toy and picked them up, put them on the side table and then packed them in her very tight suitcase. It was amazing how much clothing she carried, considering it was a nudist colony. You would have thought her beach bag was a little over the top for a supposed naked, bare all, kind of place.

Hedgy did his wiggling trick and hey presto, he had enough space to breath. He could just about move his legs and jiggle them about. That was a relief. Jeff on the other hand, felt like a sardine in a tin.

The woman's husband took the suitcases and banged them down by the reception desk, ready for their inevitable departure. Jeff and Hedgy, on the other hand, were braced for all kinds of unexpected, death threatening throws of the suitcase future bruising.

Finally, a breath of fresh air. The woman opened her suitcase and started peeling back the contents. Hedgy decided to leg it but being in one position for hours did not help his intentions. When he moved his body, his legs ached and stiffly gave him pain. Jeff, on the other hand, was moaning.

'Come on, get us out of here. I can sense intense weakness. Hedgy, you need to feed me. I'm parched. Just move, will you?'

'I'm trying. My legs don't want another journey by the pain they're telling me. You bloody walk. You bleeding, climb. You do all the leg work for a change.'

'Eeeeooooowwwww, aren't we in a mood, then.'

'You would be if you could feel my pain, Pal. Just stop going on and give us a minute, will you?'

'You've had a minute, now move.'

With that, the woman threw the top of the suitcase on top of them again.

'Now what?'

'Looks like another dark encounter with an aching, none moving hedgehog.'

'Shut the fuck up, Jeff. It's not my fault. I'm in pain, idiot.'

'If you'd have gone when I said, we would have been out of here.'

'Easy for you to say, pal.'

The room was quiet and still. The slits in the suitcase cover showed daylight along the zip line. Jeff decided he could try to get them out of there. He did some press-ups. His bell end moved the flap of the suitcase lid and after the fifty fifth time of up and down, he managed to accomplish a gap that was big enough for their escape.

'Come on Hedgy, it's your turn.'

'My turn for what, exactly?'

'To move, Dick head.'

'You're the Dick head if you remember. I'm the Dick for brains, if you recall. You're the complete Dick head, Pal.'

'Whatever. MOVE!'

'Stop ordering me about, Dick head.'

Hedgy moved little by little and eventually the stiffness and pain became less as his body slackened off. Jeff sat pretty on top of Hedgy to see all the hard work he was putting in by getting them out of there. At last, Hedgy was able to fall out of one of the sides of the suitcase walls. Then, lolled on the bed for comfort and to re-cooperate.

The woman and her husband came into the bedroom, arguing.

"Wo bist du gewesen?" ('Where have you been?')

"Nur um das Wettbüro, Warum?' ('Just to the betting office, why?')

"Ich musste helfen auspacken und sortieren diese Verwirrung aus. Ihre Mutter rief zu sagen, sie wird später kommen und über diese Wohnung ist ein Chaos. "('I needed you to help me unpack and sort this mess out. Your Mother phoned to say she is coming over later and this apartment is a mess.')

"Ich sah Fritz und er sagte mir, wir haben mehr Entlassungen bei der Arbeit." ('I saw Fritz and he told me we have more redundancies at work.')

"Ich mache dich redundant, wenn Sie wieder gehen!" ('I will make you redundant, if you go out again!')

"Nun, ich habe zu Jazz nebenan zu sehen. Ich habe versprochen, sich nennen." ('Well, I have to see Jazz next door. I promised to call in.')

"Warum? Ich brauche dich hier. "('Why? I need you here.')

He went to walk out and the woman picked up Jeff and Hedgy, wrapped in a scarf from the suitcase garments and threw them at her husband in anger as he went to vacate the bedroom. She missed him. Jeff and Hedgy flew out of the window. The scarf went one way and they forcefully, glided another. Hedgy screamed with fear. Jeff was scared but getting used to flying through the air for no apparent reason. He quite liked the tickling in his tummy and the adventure of not knowing what was going to happen next.

Doosh, thud, bounce, spring, bounce, wobble. They had landed on a canvas roof that protected the shop that was underneath the couple's apartment. It also kept the intense sunshine from hitting the shop windows. The shop was a Delicatessen. It sold all kinds of specially made German sausages that the Germans made to perfection. There was also a variety of fabulously tasting goat's cheese, bread, pretzels, Tchibo, and Dallmayr coffees, Bon bons, salami and all types of delicious meats. There were meats in the shape of sausages hanging over the counter in their masses. There was also a variety of made up hampers for seasonal selection.

The woman looked out of the window, only to see where her scarf had landed and quickly sped out of the apartment, down the hallway steps, picked up her scarf and quickly back up, grunting at her husband as he passed her leaving the building. She was fuming. She hated every bone in her husband's body but he just dismissed her abrasions as hormonal weird women's stuff. He could not wait to get away from his nagging bitch, called his woman.

Jeff and Hedgy were in an impossible dilemma. They laid on top of a canvas roof with the sun pounding heat and cooking their bodily sweat out of them. It took all of Hedgy's strength to get out of that bloody suitcase only to be landed with another problem.

'Hedgy, lie on your side, will you? My bell end is nearly cooked.'

Hedgy just did as he was told with the intensity of the heat and the desperateness of wanting water; he just succumbed to doing as asked.

They stayed turning every half an hour roughly, for at least two and a half hours in total. They received sunstroke, lashings of it. Both were very disillusioned with the pleasure of sunning yourself on a deck chair, on holiday and in the Bahamas, perhaps, where the weather suited the one thing to do. Their redness of complexion told them otherwise.

The man in the shop came out with a very large poll that he manoeuvred the canvas roof into a lid, thin pocket hole. The canvas was built into its pocket conceteaner, itself, when pushed back into its delegated area. This was just above the shop window. As the canvas moved, so did Hedgy and Jeff. It moved them into a panic of quick thinking. As The shopkeeper was getting ready to close for the rest of the day. He was also talking to passers-by. He did this particular job all day, every day, every month and every year. It almost did itself.

"Hallo Hantz, haben Sie etwas gehen billig, wie Sie Verschließen sind für diesen Abend? ('Hi Hantz, have you anything going cheap as you are closing up for this evening?')

"Nun, ja, wie in der Tat haben wir schnitzels, Bratwürste und Mayonnaise im Angebot, wenn Sie in schneller zu bekommen." ('Well, yes as a matter of fact we have schnitzels, Bratwurst sausages, and mayonnaise on offer, if you get in quick.')

The passers-by turned and shot into the shop. Another person followed. Some other customers were just leaving the premises when Hedgy and Jeff jumped and landed in a basket of goodies that was outside the shop to show passers by their sales products. They made it just in time because the canvas was slotted into its housing. The man also picked up the rest of the display baskets that cluttered the pavement all day outside.

The shop man was bearded, young at about eighteen, blond hair, brown eyes, and slender. His apron wrapped around his waist was navy blue and white wide stripes. He looked smart for a young one. It looked to be a family business. He looked to have been there forever, part of the furniture, so to speak. He was also part of a family community. He knew everybody and the community knew all there was to know about him. His history was mixed in with the locals as he worked in the shop as if he were born into it. The shop door was locked up for the night and all lights out. At last, the shop belonged to Hedgy and Jeff.

Hedgy could smell plenty of varieties to eat but all the smells were coming from above him. Jeff bent his shaft onto the dripping tap pipe not far from the floor and swung ambitiously into mid-air, then landed on the Deli counter. Hedgy was terrified, then petrified, saw the large collection of foods, and then became suddenly elated. Hedgy deliberately fell into the counter cooler. There was a humungous amount of smells, textures, feels and mouth-watering goodies to be tested and all in front of him. Hedgy gorged on Bratwurst sausages, tiny Frankfurters, the picnic variety. There was liver sausage, cut meats of all colours, textures, and flavours, smells of Smokey bacon, spread for his pleasure. He could hardly believe his eyes. Christmas had come early.

'Hedgy, for god sake, slow down. You're going to give us indigestion, in a minute. Slooowwwwww down, we've got all night.'

Hedgy took no notice and scoffed until he could scoff no more. Hedgy had taken his last bite. He could eat no more and lay between Bratwurst and liver sausage, entwined with smells of garlic sausage, which was not far away. He was over full and in heaven.

'Jeff, can we just lie here?'

'What here, in-between these smelly sausages?'

'Uuuummmmm, yup.'

'Ok then, turn to the side my friend.'

Hedgy felt Jeff flop over and he fell in line with the displayed sausages.

'It's cool in here.'

'Yes Jeff, its called a chiller. It keeps the Deli stuff cool. Hence it being called a Delicatessen!'

'Ok lard ass, know all.'

'It's nice. It's cooling my suntan nicely. Shut the fuck up and give me some peace and quiet, will you?'

Oh, all right then. End of convo, and bring in the chilling quietness.'

'You got it, pal.'

Jeff rested his weary shaft and bathed his bell end in the cool draft of the chiller breeze. He began to drift into a world of naked women all around his view. He dreamt of bouncing breasts with various nipple sizes and loved the idea of caressing every shape, size, colour, and squidgyness. Then he imagined himself just looking at huge, massive voluptuous bottoms. Tight, firm ones that creased into the thighs then disappeared into a world of beautiful mysteries. This only to be explored in private, sensually manoeuvred when asked, needed and most definitely ready and wanted. He imagined him swimming in the shallows of the blue lagoon, rubbing the crevices of their breasts with his shaft so that it tantalised his bell end sensitivity.

'Whatttttttt, what, what was that?'

'Jeff, what, what the hell was that bang?'

Jeff lifted his bell end eyes to see a shiny bright new day, and the boy man opening the canvas roof outside, that he had put away last night.

'My, I slept well. I didn't know I had fallen asleep at all.'

'Same here. Quickest sleep ever.'

An older gentleman adjusted a few items where Jeff and Hedgy were. This made the counter Deli look a little fresher, but with very little effort. Jeff and Hedgy lay like statues. They did not want attention of any kind. An old woman with a very young child came into the shop as they had just opened the shop door. She looked around and showed the young girl what was in the chiller.

The old lady turned to the salesman, "Was ist das hässlich aussehende Wurst, da?" ('What's that ugly looking sausage, there?')

She pointed to Jeff's body.

The salesman looked at her quizzically and then to what she was pointing at, 'Was, wo?" ('What, where?')

"Das gibt es." ('That there.')

"Oh, dass ummmmm. Ich weiß nicht. Ich will es loswerden. Es ist noch nicht gehören, und sieht nicht sehr appetitlich, sorry. "('Oh that, ummmmm. I don't know. I will get rid of it. It does not belong there and does not look very appetising, sorry.')

He picked Jeff and Hedgy up and took them into the back room. He put them on a pile of various meats. Then, he went back into the shop to carry on serving. The old lady asked the girl, "Möchten Sie diese oder diese zu versuchen?" ('Would you like to try those or these?')

The child said, "Ich weiß nicht, wie das Aussehen von denen. Kann ich einer von denen, bitte? "('I don't like the look of those. Can I have one of those, please?')

The Deli man replied, "Gute Wahl. Die haben ein speziell schönes Aroma. Sie mag diese Würstchen. "('Good choice. Those have an especially nice flavour. You'll like these Frankfurters.')

The old lady smiled and said to the salesman, "Ja, bitte fünf und zwei große Bocwurst. Oh, und haben Sie irgendwelche Sauerkraut? ('Yes, five please and two large Bocwurst. Oh and have you any sauerkraut?')

"Ja Frau Kouhler. Wie viele? '('Yes Mrs Kouhler. How many?')

"Nur die ein Glas, danke." ('Just the one jar, thank you.')

Mrs Kohler and the little girl said their thanks and good byes. On the way out the old woman spoke kindly to the young man working outside the shop and left to visit another day.

The salesman came to where he had put Jeff and Hedgy and switched on the mincing machine that was grinding round and round. The noise was loud and the horror was mind blowing. Jeff and Hedgy had assessed their predicament and decided if they did not move now, they would be possibly the next chopped liver sausage or stuck in a pie or some other German culinary tasty delight. That made them decide to live and so frighteningly so. They desperately needed to get out of there.

The man went to get some more meat for his new creations. Hedgy, abruptly got to his feet, ran down the mound of dead flesh, and then jumped onto the floor. Jeff quickly assessed the area and told Hedgy to run for the back door that was open in the corner of the room. Hedgy did not have to be told twice. He legged it as fast as he possibly could. The salesman did not even know they had been in his shop. They hid behind some large, plastic containers.

'That was bloody close.'

'Let's get out of here.'

The streets of Germany were so clean, no rubbish. Even the net curtains were regimentally pinned in pristine lines of flowing immaculateness. All garden gates closed and all gardens regimented with beautiful flowers, borders and each blade of grass cut to a specific length and height. The whole street was a creative pattern of smartness and of individualized design.

As they walked, they came across public garden areas that had been very, very carefully thought out and executed for the purpose of spectacular displays along with practicalities for the public to not spoil. On their travels, there was a river. It flowed gently and shallow. The babbling brook was not only clear but you could swim in it. You could see creatures such as tiny fish of all shapes and colours, just enjoying their environment with no interference from the outside world. Crayfish keeping in the shadows and going on with their natural happy go lucky habitat, again with no interference.

The fresh twinkling of the clear waters looked inviting, mesmerising, a television of stories from the wild nature to be captivated and treasured forever whispered and shared with all who took a snap shot with them.

Hedgy walked for miles enjoying the open countryside. They took in a way of life strange in looks, smells, layout and heard the occasional German language spoken with or without an accent from each area passed. Either way, it did not matter because they could not speak or understand any of it. In fact, most of the places they visited spoke gobbledy gook for that reason alone.

It was dark. They reached a tiny village. There were plenty of shops that were closed for the night and in no particular area, there were tables and benches. Hedgy decided to kip under the benches for the rest of their stay. It was pleasant, peaceful, dry and most of all cool. Next morning, they heard the hustle and bustle of market stallers fixing, changing, and creating their goods for the shoppers to be wowed into buying their wares. There were wonderful collections of dolls, antiques, sweets, food, specially prepared and others to take home, wrapped up. All were made in Germany.

The public house where they slept was open for cleaning, organising, and getting ready for prospective customers. They wanted people to sup and be merry, all day and into the night. The women would shop until they dropped at the market and shops around. The men folk would drink while their family shopped and after more supping, the family would join their merriment.

Jeff suddenly got excited. Women, bar maids with chests spilling over, under their necks. They had traditional German Pub uniforms on. That meant elasticated and drawstring chest cover in crisp, clean bright, white, and bodice in black. It had a criss-cross ribbon on the front to the skirt that flared, just under the knees. The sleeves were short, puffed elasticated, white, clean, and crisp to match their chests. Their beautiful hairs were mostly, traditionally platted with more ribbon of the same colour that was on the dress. Some women had blond, short hair and other red that kicked tradition out of the window to modern times. Either way, beer festivals were rife and they were certainly in the right place for a good old knees up but only if nobody noticed Hedgy and Jeff under the tables.

It took hours for the festival to open and finally at about ten late morning, people started arriving. Families gathered in jolliment and the atmosphere spread over the whole of the village.

Jeff could only admire and wonder what pleasure he could show all his girls that were dressed so Moorish. He wanted to get to know each one individually, have his wicked way, naughty and nice pleasure, with one, and then move onto his next adorable, hopeful, want to get to know him more victims. All he could think was his hardest challenge yet and that was sexual encounters with every last one of those beauties.

The festival began. The live band pounded English sounds. The beer spilled in puddles all around Hedgy and some on Jeff. The alcohol, even though not very strong, soaked into Jeff and Hedgy's body. A girl dropped her headband that landed on Jeff's bell end. He proudly wore a very new bandana of German colours around the top of his bell end.

Hedgy heard a Talking Heads number (Road to Nowhere) and started dancing on two back legs to it. Jeff joined in the song and between them joined the rowdy crowd of nonsensical droning of gobbledy gook. Hedgy and Jeff drank heavily into the night. Their senses, what senses? Each one had very little to no ability to work properly at all. Their bodies were so intoxicated, they swayed in different directions. Their singing ability had definitely diminished into proper gobbledy gook and they did not give a shit about anything or anyone. The people around them were so paralytically happy they did not even acknowledge a penis on a hedgehog underneath their seats. It had gone past the stage of clarity and just became a free for all.

Jeff woke up next day and felt a great big blister on the top of his knob. Hedgy had the hangover from hell. His eyes hurt when lifting his head and adjusted for daylight. He thought he tasted a bratwurst sausage that was just about to regurgitate but went down just in time. No, it came up again and into a nearby drain. He thought, that was lucky. Jeff was still pissed and crying, 'where are my lovely girlies. There gone. Somebody took them from me.'

Hedgy said nothing and tried to curl up in a preserving hedgehog ball, but could not because of Jeff's skin grafted meld.

Time ticked its quiet clock over badly and the noise came tumbling down after. Jeff thought to himself, does anything at all work our way, or are we jinxed? Are our lives always to be going to be so shitty? Hedgy also thought that if he did have a guardian angel, then he or she does not know how to play the game or new to its guardianship and or is just bloody minded to give a shit.

Jeff, still drunk shouted for no apparent reason, 'give us a fucking break, you fuckers.'

Hedgy just after, shouted, 'Yeah give us a fucking break you inadequate pieces of shit. Go get a paper job and leave us alone.'

They're both looked peculiarly at each other and understood nothing. All they could do was slouch, close their eyes and sleep. All Jeff could do was try and put his blistering knob in some kind of comfortable position, which was nigh on impossible.

A woman with black teeth picked them up and stroked, whilst cuddling Jeff. He shouted, 'Hedgy, get me out of here. Witch, put me down. I'm not that kind of prick and you're not my type.'

Hedgy was fast asleep and snoring as his usual deep sleep was in motion.

Jeff just kept shouting, 'Hedgy, Hedgy!'

Nobody was interested in Jeff's nightmare and left it to him. Hedgy woke up late in the afternoon. It must have been a Sunday because all the shops were closed and the hustle and bustle of shopping was not.

CRATED

Jeff and Hedgy lived life to the full. Drinking and singing, singing and drinking, then eating. After roughly a month, Hedgy was getting bored with his lot and Jeff was becoming a drunk, irritable and downright horrid with his mood swings. Hedgy had no choice; he was stuck with a pure dick head attached to his otherwise healthy body.

One night hedgy deliberately smacked Jeff's body into the side of the wooden bench hoping he would just fall off. Jeff smacked his bell end so hard that he was concussed and woke up from a beautiful, drunken deep sleep.

'What the hell was that?'

'Sorry, just turned over to get comfortable.'

'Wow, my head nearly came off. Did you do that deliberately?'

'No, go to sleep.'

'Yes you did.'

'No I bloody didn't.'

'Yes you fucking did, you dick shite.'

It was obvious, Jeff was still bladdered and started singing, 'woof the magic draaaagon lived by the tree, Frolicked in the riverbed in a land of one, two tree.'

'You've got the words wrong. It's not woof, its puff and it's not tree, its sea. Annddd......'

'No its not. Anyway, that's my version.'

'Try singing it properly, if you don't mind.'

'No, gob shite, I won't.

'Ok Jeff, yes I did deliberately try to knock your fucking head off.'

'See I told you.'

'I want to get rid of you for good.'

'But why? You're my bestist friend in the whole wide world. My secrets, you know all my secrets. You know me inside out.'

'Yes and I hate every bone in your cocking body.'

'I don't have any of those, Hedgy.'

'Well you know what I mean. You are irritating, abusive, argumentative, outrageously horrid, and fucking loud.'

'AND?'

'What D'you mean AND?'

'Don't you love me anymore, then?'

'No I fucking don't. I want to get out of here on my own. Find my own way home and enjoy the rest of my life, shagging hedgehogs, eating slugs and talking to my own kind.'

'Well that's nice innit. I give you adventures of a life time and you are rude, nasty, and brutal to your one and only friend.'

'Oh, go back to sleep, you bullshitter.'

Hedgy just got up and walked. He did not care what Jeff was doing. He only felt his body swaying back and forth as Hedgy marched to the road ahead. Hedgy walked with anger and stormed down the road with such vigour, speed, and adamants in his approach to life in general.

Hedgy was walking and his legs were stretching the air. He tried without a prayer to put his feet upon the ground he had just trod. He looked up realising something was definitely wrong. Holding Jeff's blistered bell end was a cow. It had bent down and put its mouth around Jeff. Jeff felt pain of the blister and shouted, 'ouch, put me down. You've burst my blister. You've burst my blister.'

Hedgy still trying to walk the air on all fours replied, 'the bloody cow did it.'

'Huh?'

'You are now in the mouth of a cow. You lucky prick.'

'Owe, he's burst my blister, and it bloody hurts. Oi, cow put me down.'

'That's no way to talk to somebody chewing the cud, ha, ha, ha, ha.'

'Ouch it's chewing my bloody blister.'

'Yes I told you, the cud, ha, ha, ha. You always did have fluid on the brain.'

Jeff struggled from side to side and eventually the cow got the message. It let go and ran off. Another cow attempted to pick Jeff up but another cow pushed him away, wanting to get a look in. Hedgy fell to the ground and got covered in mud, or was it cow pat shit.

'Noooooo, cow pat shite.'

'Phew, you dun arf stink, Hedgy.'

'Why is it I always get the worst end of it?'

'Because you is the man, my friend. You is the hedge man.'

Jeff could see no end to cows coming his way so he wrapped his bell end around one of the available cow tails dangling for his convenience. It stank. It was full of flaky, smelly, dried stench. The cow flicked its tail and Hedgy got a mouthful of cow pat shite. He started choking, coughing, and spluttering.

'Owe, yuk, cough, cough, spit, spit, spit, choke.'

'Hedgy, I will get you out of this, you watch me.'

Rambo had arrived and swung from one cow tail to the next to the next and then fell in a cowpat. Both were covered at every orifice. Words failed Hedgy. He just sat, belly, legs and chin in dung, smelly horrible dung.

The cows had been called into a loading lorry. They slowly walked into the death wagon awaiting their travel to doom. A cow that was behind them stood for a couple of seconds and Jeff managed to wrap himself again, around the tail of a calf. The calf bolted and ran to the far field. The farmer was also taking the calf to market and rounded all into his carrying wagon. Jeff was able to bend into the tail and secure his position while travelling. They were driven for miles and about an hour or two. When they arrived, the cows were let into a holding pen ready to be sold at market for later that day. Jeff was still holding on to the calf's tail and was looking for a safe place to drop.

'Hedgy, when I say drop, you get ready to fall on the floor, ok?'

'All right.'

Hedgy's body of cowpat and mud had hardened like a face pack. Every time he moved one of his feet, something flaky fell off.

'One, two, noo.'

'Come on stop messing about.'

'One two three, jump.'

Hedgy crushed his flaking kneecaps as he thudded to the ground. The stiffness fell apart and he legged it to the nearest hide away, dark spot of the market place. There were corrugated walls and gaps all on one side of the cows holding pen. Hedgy squeezed into one of them. They just sat there, listening to every footpstep, noise, and shuffle. Eventually, Jeff peered out and noticed the holding pen had been emptied that the cows were put in. Other holding pens had goats, smelly horribly, dirty, jumping goats. Another had very small, dumpy miniature pigs with speckles on. At the other end, a collection of pens with sheep in.

They slept the night behind the corrugated walls and early next morning tried to escape to the road again. At the same time some, tiny speckled pigs arrived and were put into the holding pen where Jeff and Hedgy were trying to get through for their new road venture. A pig grunted, 'where the hell you pair going?'

Hedgy said nothing. Jeff on the other hand replied, 'what's it to you?'

'You are in my pen, so what you doing in my pen?'

'We are trying to escape and hit the road.'

'I wouldn't if I were you.'

'Well I'm not you and let us through.'

'Be my guest. Your call.'

Jeff thought it odd to say but told Hedgy to carry on all the same.

'Move Hedgy, run.'

The pig started to squeal, pop and click, like a pig in agony. All punters eyes was on that area to see what all the commotion was about.

'Squeal, you won't get far. Squeal, they're coming for you. Squeal, you have not got a chance.'

Hedgy ran around in a circle and around the pig in question. He could see no way out. Panic struck and hedgy crawled into a corner. They were picked up by a farmer and put into a small station wagon.

'Dam, now what?'

Jeff, what now. How do we get out of here?'

They waited roughly twenty minutes. The farmer put the pigs that he had won at auction, in the back of the truck. The cage was small for three little pigs. The farmer checked that Hedgy and Jeff were still in the station wagon and then got in and drove off.

'Hey stinking pigs, why did you do that?'

'Did what?'

'You squealed on us.'

'Well you were in our pen.'

'I was trying to get out.'

'Well you were in our pen.'

'You could have just kept quiet and let us just be on our way.'

'Ummm yup, I could have done but then we would not be talking to you now, would we.'

'You mean you drew attention to us so that you could have a bit of company?'

'Here's looking at you kid.'

'I am not a bloody kid and I think you are awful doing that to us.'

'Look we are going to, we don't know where, to live with who we don't know and to a prison we don't know why. We learnt a long time ago that we are only on this dam earth once, so we decided to spend as much time with other creatures as long as we possibly could. For us, life really is too short. Them there humans like our bodies and slaughter our young as quick as we make them. So we want enjoyment in our lives and meeting people like you gives us a buzz. You thank your lucky stars cos we will be put in cages and will not be able to move ever again until we die. So pardon me for trying to talk to somebody for a little light entertainment.'

'Sorry pal, we didn't know. My names Hedgy and sitting on top of me is Jeff.'

'Sitting on top of what?'

'On top of me is my friend Jeff.'

Jeff was startled, happy and almost wanted to cry, 'you called me friend. That means you love me, need me, want me, and care.'

'Ok, don't push it.'

The pig said, 'what kind of friend is he?'

'He's a human penis friend that got attached whilst in a ditch in England.'

'How the hell did that come about, then?'

'He was in a car crash and got, well, chopped off.'

'Why can't he tell us?'

'Because he has no mouth, only eyes, which are blurry with alcohol these days.'

Jeff got angry at his afflictions and said, 'just stick to the nice bits will you.'

'It's a blessing he can't talk because he wouldn't shut up otherwise.'

Jeff started wriggling and became a nuisance.

'Is that the way he communicates then?'

'Uuuummmm sort of. Jeff, stop playing up. Be a nice Dick for a change, will you?'

'Well, stop taking the piss then.'

'He can be a nice penis when he wants to be.'

Everybody settled into their long journey ahead. Finally, they reached an airport. It was the kind that did cargo trips in small quantities. The farmer found a small wooden carrying box for Hedgy and Jeff to be sent in. He also heard the farmer speak in German saying, "Ich habe einen Sonderfall für Sie. Es ist live und konnte in den Kollektionen als etwas anderes hinzugefügt. "('I have a special case for you. It is live and could be added to your collections as something different.')

He then chuckled and walked off putting the phone away in his overall pocket.

Hedgy tried to bite the farmer because he was scared and did not like his tone. The farmer gave him a whack and sealed him into the crate. Later, Hedgy heard the pigs squealing and shouted, 'where you going?'

'They are putting us onto a small plane. I should imagine you will be coming too.'

'Oh, well see you later then?'

The pig shouted, 'all right then. Look forward to it.'

Hedgy and Jeff just sat and sat and sat. Finally, the crate with them in it was lifted and carried to the pig plane and put on the backside of the aircraft to travel without being knocked over. Jeff heard the Russian pilot say, "Это собирается принять около пяти часов, потому что мы должны остановиться в России. У меня есть больше груза, чтобы взять в Японию ". ('It's going to take about five hours because we need to stop off in Russia. I have more cargo to take to Japan.')

'Hedgy, did you understand any of that garble?'

'No Jeff, I heard nothing I could put my finger on. We had better just sit tight and enjoy the ride, then.'

'Ok guys, planet Mars it is then. Take me away from all this.'

'Tally hoooooo and bollocks to Noddy.'

The Russian farmer climbed into the plane and sat on one of the front passenger seats. The captain made one last check that everything and everyone was secure and safe to go. There was a thud, and then a click, then the engine roared after twenty seconds or so.

The pigs squealed in horror the noise was horrifically loud. Jeff and Hedgy cowered down. The plane lifted and shuddered. It felt very rickety and swayed from side to side, as it swept the sky on ascending. You could almost feel the air fighting against the pressure of the airstreams and when reaching the clouds, it almost rested into submission as it petered out into a balance of equal weight as its wings forced the elements to do as they were told.

Riding high had its momentum and the stomach had its disagreements. One minute you could feel the force, the next you could feel the pressure and the next your ears felt clogged with air space. Either way they did not feel normal.

They hit an air pocket and dipped out of balance. The nose of the plane wanted to see the distant ground below and then the pilot insisted they ride above the cloud. It was up and down, up and down for quite a few miles.

Jeff's knob was throbbing and asked Hedgy, 'D'you think my knob is going to fall off or something?'

'Well, it could be infected or just plain sore.'

'Oh yes, I get the pun. Plane sore. Yes got it.'

'Hedgy nearly rolled around the crate in laughter but did not have much room.

'Hedgy, be serious. Do you think my blister will get infected, burst and then my knob will drop off, cos it's very sore, indeed?'

'Well, you can keep a close eye on it and if it does drop off; you can watch it, can't you.'

'You are no help at all, are you?'

The pig was listening and asked Jeff to bend forward so he could have a look at his blistered Penis head.

'I think it looks a little angry and you could do with a dose of mud on it.'

'Mud, mud, bloody mud. Did you hear this fat bellied fuck whit?'

'No, I'm being serious. We use mud if we have an open wound and it works for all of us.'

Each one said, 'yes, yes and yes.'

'Ok pal, do I look like a pig.'

Hedgy said, 'No you look like a prick.'

'No you need talent, charisma, poise, elegance, and pulling power to look like one of us. Between you and me you got nothing, so don't even think about competing, pal.'

'Competing with what, you lot? You must be joking. There is no comparison, pal.'

Hedgy was hurting from listening and laughing. He said nothing just carried on listening to the entertainment on board.

Jeff was fuming with all the insulting remarks thrown into his cage. There was no escape and he could not think of anything else to say, so he just sat and sulked. The pigs stopped making noises and all eventually fell asleep with the momentum and pressure of being in the air.

The jerky plane took a dive to another level and woke everybody up.

'Wow, what's going on.'

'Ummmmm, I think they are getting ready to land.'

The pilot shouted back at them, 'поставить ремень безопасности и убедитесь, что весь груз привязали вниз, не так ли? "('Put your seat belt on and make sure all the cargo is strapped down, will you?')

The farmer rocked from side to side, was shocked at the swaying of the aircraft, and replied, "Я рад, да, я проверю. Как скоро мы приземлимся? 'Yes, yes, (I will check. How long before we land?')

"Оооо, около десяти минут. Теперь уже недолго. Пусть ваши паспорта готовы к проверке ". ('Ooohhh, about ten minutes. Not long now. Have your passports ready for inspection.')

The farmer made sure all was tied down. He then checked in his pocket for documentation that he would need for him and his pigs. He did not need anything for Jeff and Hedgy, he thought.

The wheels screeched the tarmac and bumped along the runway. The force could be felt and the powerful pressure to halt the plane was feeling very strong. It was a tug of war and eventually, the pilot won with his determination. He knew what he was doing and with his might, you could also feel the experience and knowhow of the man at the controls.

All tension was released and breath was inhaled when they could see the plane had stopped on the runway.

'This is the most frightening thing I have ever had to be involved in, Hedgy.'

'Me too, Jeff. You all right?'

The pigs squealed on touch down and didn't stop until the plane came to a halt. The pig said, 'Get me out of here. I want a weeee. Oohhhh, too late.'

Another pig replied, 'yes on my foot, you oaf.'

'Well, they've certainly got something in common with you Jeff, haven't they?'

'And what's that may I ask?'

'You like pissing on peoples heads, don't you?'

The pig answered, 'You didn't?'

Before Jeff could answer Hedgy replied, 'yes and Jeff also thought it would be good for me because it was warm.'

The pigs squealed with laughter and thought it so ridiculously funny.

'I did not think it amusing at all. In fact, I thought it disgusting.'

'Well, what are friends for then Jeff? Huh, huh?'

JAPANESE GEISHA DOLLS FOR YOUR PLEASURE

The time had arrived for the plane to take off again. The Russian pilot had refuelled and the farmer had been told by security, that he had not needed to show his credentials because they were not stopping. Security checked the crates and did not know what to make of Jeff and Hedgy. Either way, they just wanted all of them in the sky so they did not have to bother with a peculiar Hedgy and his piggy mates. Incidentally, the pigs squealing got on everyone's nerves and they were glad to see the back of them.

The engine roared. The pigs squealed and the farmer too.

'Jeff, D'you know where we are going now?'

'Haven't a clue.'

One of the pigs heard their conversation and butted in, 'well, on your crate it's printed JA, PAN.'

'Why Japan?'

The pig chuckled, 'I don't know but if you're going then so are we.'

'Have you ever been there?'

'No, never but if that's the place we're gonna end up, then I might as well commit hari-kari now.'

'Why?'

'They treat all animals as if they are nothing. No sense no feeling. They torture and eat anything that moves. Even you need to watch your back.'

'What, why us?'

'Why not? You are edible, just like the rest of us. Meat is meat. It just comes in different disguises.'

Jeff heard all and became very anxious about his life before him.

'Hedgy, you need to get us out of here. I mean it. They're not eating me alive nor cutting my cock up for somebody to gnaw on. Suck, yes, gnaw, nooooo way.'

'You get us out of here. I'm sick of doing it. You find a way.'

'D'you want to live or not?'

One of the pigs squealed, yes, take us with you, please, please, please, take us with you?'

'Hedgy, you heard. You are in demand and it is your job, but I am your guide.'

'Bloody guide. You couldn't guide a cock roach into a paper bag.

'I thought I did very well getting us out of the Beer Cellar Bar in Germany.'

'What, you were so pissed your dick scraped the floor with your blister and I carried you to here.'

'Yes and what a mess you got us into, pal.'

'Don't you Pal me. You've been drunk for weeks and have the audacity to ask me to help you. Dream on, doughnut.'

The pigs all squealed, 'Hedgy please, you're our last hope. Come on we need you. We are begging you save us from the Japanese.'

'Hedgy, sorry Pal. We need you, now more than ever.'

The Russian Farmer was fed up of the squealing and in his native tongue told them all to shut up. He was also angry and banged on all the crates, then sat back in his seat with eyebrows growling and arms folded in his gruff stance, which meant I am an unhappy chappy, stiff position.

The pressure was on and Hedgy knew he was being forced into a position that he just did not know how to get out of. He was worried, very worried because he could not think of any plan, what so ever.

'Ok guys, be ready to go when I say because opportunity strikes in unusual ways and I'm not sure when ours will.'

'That's not a plan and how you going to do this? Look, when the plane doors open we will just run for it.'

'Oh yes, and what about the crate of wood surrounding our departure? Oh I get it, me and thee will just hop through hoops for you, shall we? And, while we are on the subject of idioticness, stay out of my way.'

'My knob hurts.'

'If you are trying for the sympathy vote, you can kiss my butt, pal.'

Jeff was lost for words and his blister was infected. His bell end was red, enflamed, and over sensitive with pain. Jeff just sat still and sulked. The piggies settled down, the plane tail lifted, and the pressure experience started all over again. This time there was no squealing due to the sensations were all known by all.

The journey took up more hours than before and the landing just as uncomfortable as the first.

By the time they got there and touched down, it was dark and raining hard. The dank, dark breeze of an oriental place was scary.

The pigs knew the danger they were in every second of being caged and vulnerable. Their future looked grim, very grim.

The farmer handed over the money owed, chatted awhile, and ran, leaving all in the plane. Later, when he came back he came with two other men and a four-wheeler truck.

One of the men checked documentations and cargo. When it came to Jeff and Hedgy, a great big analysis of what, how, why and when was questioned. Jeff could understand nothing but saw many hands went up in the air, frowns, laughs and so many communicative gestures. After wearing themselves out talking, the man and the farmer turned to the pigs, again discussed, and analysed all over again. Hedgy was getting agitated because all he wanted to do was get them out of there, but with the man and the farmer having a good old conversation; it was obviously an impossible time for them to create any distraction for an attempted escape at that moment in time.

At last, some men came and carried the crate of pigs to the Farmers truck. Next, it was Jeff and Hedgy's turn. Hedgy was not going without a fight and screeched, 'let me go. I want to go home. I don't deserve to die. Hey, hey, hey, listen let me go, you Russian shite, tit!'

The Farmer banged on the top of the crates and instantly got a fierce, shut up reaction. The crate was picked up and handled only by the Russian Farmer.

The crates were taken. The door of the plane closed and slowly disappeared under a specially made dome where aeroplanes lived.

Once they were all in the truck, the Farmer drove into Japan's motorways until the roads narrowed and the buildings nearly touched the vehicles on both sides. Small streets, bright lights and squashed residential habitats, went on for miles until they reached a crossroads.

The rain never gave up. In fact, it became torrential. The truck stopped and a few tiny squeaks could be heard from the back of the vehicle.

'Hedgy, is it time yet?'

'For what?'

'You know, to escape.'

'Shh, keep the noise down.'

Jeff kept very still and said absolutely nothing.

'Well, 'the piggies whispered, 'well, is it now?'

'Nooo, shut up. I need to think. No, can't you see the rain, its pelting down.'

'Later then?'

'Yes, later when we get out of this truck. In the meantime, don't upset the Farmer.'

'Jeff, you're quiet. Blister got your tongue, then?'

'You are the most horridist Hedgehog that went to the University of Horridness, you are.'

'There, there. I was only joking. Just like you do, pal.'

'I'm not that horrid.'

'Oohh yes you are. You're worse.'

'And how D'you work that out?'

'Because you simply are.'

'My cock hurts Hedgy, really hurts.'

'Sorry mate, I can't do anything from here. You will just have to wait.'

'I just feel so shit, Hedgy.'

After ten minutes or so, the rain gave up, the clouds moved for a pitch-black cloudless sky. The Farmer started the engine and drove carefully through a road of mud, potholes, and guesswork. On both sides of the plain, you could see squares of paddy fields, with hints of glistening water ripples.

The truck reached a hut house with a huge bump and twist of the wheels, hitting sludge and uneven grassed ditches.

'Hedgy.'

'What?'

'D'you really think I've got knob rot?'

'Don't be stupid.'

'Brain rot more like.'

One of the pigs oinked, 'what's knob rot?'

'Don't start him off.'

'Well, you see it's like this. Shut up Hedgy. When we landed in Crete we ended up on an Island called Spinalonga. This Islands people all had leprosy.'

'What's Leprosy?'

'What's Spinalonga?'

'Where's the Farmer gone?'

'How we going to get out of here?'

'For god sake, one at a time. I can't think.'

Hedgy butted in, 'Spinalonga (leprosarium) is a small Island of Crete in Greece. It was once inhabited at one time by a colony of lepers. Leprosy, also known as Hansen's disease, is a flesh rotting disease, which breaks down the tissues of the skin, starts on the fingers and toes, then the eyes, and smells like rotting meat. The wounds are open to infection. It is a deteriorating and debilitating disease in not treated, that is a bacterium and still exists today. They were put on Spinalonga, deliberately because the disease then had no cure and even today they do not know where it came from. Now they have found a cure. To answer your question, Jeff has an infected blister and not leprosy.'

'Well that makes me feel better. NOT.'

The Farmer and his helper came back absolutely dripping wet through. They both grabbed each side of the pigs crate and picked it up to put it down just outside on the ground. As they did so, one of them slipped and the crate hit the deck. The pigs squashed against each other and fell out of the crack on the crate wall. The squealing was intense. Panic set in and the pigs dispersed in all directions. The Farmer and his helper spread their arms out to try to confine the pigs from running away but it did not work. The opportunity had been gifted and the present taken. They dashed in mud, grass, and ran hell for leather in any direction, just to escape.

All Jeff and Hedgy could do was watch enviously on, anticipating their getaway.

The Farmer caught nothing but more rain and both fell in mud. They were so angry that the pigs got away. They were also extremely careful with Jeff and Hedgy's crate. They were not going to get any optimistic luck any time soon for escaping.

The Russian Farmer carried their crate on his own and told his helper to find the pigs but not come back until he had.

The hut house was very basic with a hole in the middle of the room for cooking and heating. In addition, a couple of wooden slatted makeshift beds to sit on as chairs. Jeff and Hedgy were put in a dark part of the room. They were chilled to the bone and took ages to warm up. Jeff realised he had lost his bandana. Eventually, they drifted into a few hours' sleep.

Jeff woke up with the sound of children. One poked through the cage to wake up Hedgy.

'Oi, oi, no poking. Leave me alone. I want to stay cold, wet, damp and in a coma.'

He hissed, popped, clicked, at them and they stepped back with surprise. Jeff banged against the wood and wished he hadn't. His knob was still swollen, red, and tender. His bell end was throbbing. Hedgy heard the children come back for inquisitive play. They moved when they pointed and pushed at them; so what more could they do to get another reaction?

The Russian Farmer had a social meal with his family and left at about mid-evening. Jeff and Hedgy were examined, laughed at, prodded, and poked by at least twenty people all told.

'I'm getting sick of this. I am going to take no notice, play dead, and then they might realise we need feeding too.'

'I'm dying, Hedgy. The pain is unbearable.'

One of the women took the lid off the crate and grabbed Jeff's shaft. He squealed like no animal on earth but nobody heard his anguish. She put them on the table where light shone the most and examined both Jeff and Hedgy. The woman then touched and analysed Jeff's knob. His eyes opened and she could see that Jeff was alive as well as Hedgy, who was still hissing and squealing. She put some kind of sticky substance on his blistered, throbbing knob after discussing with other members of the family. If Jeff could have hit the roof with his stinging pain, he would have. He wriggled in agony to try to get away from pure torment but to no advantage. The more he wriggled, the more it hurt. The faces of the women were of worry, frustration, and determination. One of the little girls came over sobbing. Her mother cuddled her distraught daughter, whilst another woman put a makeshift bandage around Jeff; making sure his bell end was covered.

'Hedgy, Jeff cried out, 'get us the hell out of here. They're killing me slowly. This has got to be the worst torture ever. I would rather be boiled alive like that frog's lover in the Caribbean than suffer this. Please Hedgy, please?'

Hedgy felt useless. He wanted to help his pain in the arse friend and just leg it but there were too many people ready to pounce if they attempted to escape. In addition, the grip of the adults holding them down to the table was over powering. A long tube was put over Jeff's make shift bandage. He could do nothing because only just be there for his mate. Hedgy said nothing because nothing was thinking and nothing was giving him the right answers. Nothing could actually be done but bide their time and hope.

Jeff and Hedgy were finally put back in their new home, the crate. A bowl of water was placed by Hedgy, which he drank like no tomorrow. Also, a dish of rice was placed next to the water. Nothing lasted with Hedgy; he ate so fast he was given more food until he could chomp no more.

The children entertained Jeff and Hedgy. They also fed and watered Hedgy, which made him soften to their interests. Jeff and Hedgy were treated like the children's pet. The adults made sure the children did their poo's and wee's, plus the cleaning and entertained their newly found friends.

A week later, they were taken out of the crate and the bandages were carefully taken off. Jeff had not complained once of pain, nor had he moaned about anything to Hedgy, just left him alone, guilty that he could not help his friend in his desperate hour of need. His blister had nearly gone and the swelling had completely gone down. Jeff stood there erect and willing for intervention. He knew after his week long experience that these people were not going to eat them, boil them, bake them or harm them, but help them get better. Jeff was also washed very carefully with some kind of oil. This he thought, was very pleasurable, and became most aroused. She stopped just as he was about to explode his essence. She then put the cardboard tube back on Jeff's shaft. Jeff and Hedgy were quite relieved to go back in their new home because the children played innocently rough sometimes but mostly kindly. Once or twice, they prodded Hedgy's feet to make him dance and thought it funny. Other times put him in a handmade cart with wheels and pushed the cart into the door for decapitation. Hedgy moved surprisingly quickly and Jeff was saved by the cardboard being so stiff, when his body hit the wooden bars on the bed frame. All in all, they were fearful of all the tykes that lived there. They just did not have a clue how to look after another living creature. For some reason all children were dressed as Geisha girls, which meant heavily painted white make-up faces, hair put in a Japanese style, and traditionally jewelled. The dresses were eloquently wrapped in a traditional special way and the shoes were made of painted wood with two pieces of paralleled painted the same, heel to give height. The boys wore something different altogether. One was a dragon with an elongated, huge frightful multi-coloured dragonhead and attached to his body with another boy with sticks to manipulate the tail to give it a sense of life and movement. The next was somewhat obscure. It looked like some kind of demon. The rest of the family had masks that matched the colours of their costumes.

Jeff and Hedgy were put on the dining table. One of the older girls knew about Jeff being alive and took his cardboard tube off. She looked pleased.

'Hedgy, tell me what they're doing?'

'I think your knob has healed. How does it feel?'

'Wellll, yes, I think my leprosy has healed. I really do.'

'Bloody leprosy, you never had it. You had a feckin blister, for god sake.'

'All right, all right, calm down, it's my knob, and I can have what I want. Got it!'

'No I haven't got anything. You have.'

'And what's that?'

Hedgy went to run off the table and was caught in mid-air by one of the older children. He squealed like a pig almost and tried to bite the girl's finger. He was promptly put back onto the table and held down with a cloth of sorts.

'What the hell did you do that for?'

'Element of surprise, Jeff. Element of surprise. But it didn't feckin work, did it.'

'Calm down Hedgy. We're safe that's the main thing.'

'Safe, safe, feckin, floppin, fuckin safe? I don't want to be safe. I want to be out of here. All that poking and prodding. Those kids are driving me crazy and you're not helping.'

'Yes Hedgy. I will shut the fuck up, ok?'

'You got it, Pal.'

Once all had calmed down then the dress code began. A long kitchen roll was put on Jeff's shaft. It was taken off again, holes put in for Jeff's eyes to see through and gently put back on so that he could see through the holes. Hedgy just sat there in a grump and let them do what they wanted. Jeff was dressed as a Samurai Warrior.

'Watch where you're swinging that sword, will you?'

'What sword?'

'The one they've just tied to you.'

'Oh, that plastic monstrosity of a knife?'

'No, that rip a bollock off, bastard sheath of metal, spinning next to my head.'

'Look, I didn't attach the ruddy thing, they did.'

Hedgy stopped squeaking at Jeff and they were dressed almost ready for action.

'D'you know what they're dressing us up for?'

'Haven't a clue.'

Jeff and Hedgy were put in an enclosed box. Then went on a bumpy ride for ages. The children were over excited and so to, were the adults. When the truck stopped all got out and Jeff and Hedgy were carried in the box into an ornate fancy carved building. It was painted primarily in black, red trimmings with lashings of gold exhibits. The theatre was over full and they struggled to get through the crowd. Jeff and Hedgy were held high and passed over the family until they reached their private room.

The chaotic family got themselves organised. The adults walked on stage and acted out their part of the play. It was a combination of acting and miming. One of the women sang a Ballard and some men mimed aggressively toward each other as if to fight. Next, the children in masks went on and two of the boys were dressed similar to Jeff in their Samurai uniforms. Hedgy was put on the ground and a collar put around Jeff's bollocks. The middle boy held them down until it was time to perform. The boy let go and Hedgy was pulled behind the children. The boys fought the enemy and the smaller Samurai stood by Hedgy and Jeff. A boy put his sword as if to stab Hedgy and was pulled onto his side, as if to die. The curtain closed as the crowd clapped with appreciation.

The next time the curtain opened, they saw the Geisha girls in all their glory. Later, came the dragon, then the bad guy and more masked actors. Hedgy and Jeff were held the whole time but were so engrossed in what was going on, they just soaked up the whole evenings experiences. Escaping never entered their heads.

The night was a total success for the Japanese community. The jollyment flowed all the way home. Jeff and Hedgy were put on the end of one of the children's bed and everyone went to sleep. They were worn out and all slept cool right through the night.

Jeff had woken up by somebodies feet pushing him slightly further down the bed. He was just about to go back to sleep when Hedgy twitched his nose and quietly said, 'I don't want to escape. I like these creatures and come to know them as our friends.'

'Me neither but we must get out of here.'

Hedgy gently slid sideways. Jeff was erect and alert. Hedgy put two feet on the ground and fell off the bed with a clonk. Jeff quickly adjusted himself to look if anyone had heard or noticed them but nobody did. The family tossed and turned but did not wake. After an agonising minute Hedgy moved towards the one and only door. The breeze could be felt through the gaps of wood at the bottom, broken off in gaps from abuse over time. Hedgy whispered, 'can you squeeze through that one?'

Jeff whispered back, 'no, it's not big enough.'

'Just punch it, it will break.'

'I'll break your bloody head in a minute. Stop pushing me.'

The door opened briskly. Jeff and Hedgy were suddenly squashed behind it. The Russian Farmer stood there and that woke some of the adults. It was nearly dawn and the Farmer let the sun in. Hedgy adjusted his stance and assessed their situation. One good thing in that was, nobody had seen or heard them go. The Farmer stepped forward. Jeff and Hedgy spun into action, behind the farmer at the door and just missed the door slamming behind them.

'Phewwwww. That was close.'

'Look, no mud and its beautiful out here.'

It was the first time they had seen outside without being in a crate, box, in fact anything. The breeze was fresh and the atmosphere calm.

'Do we have to go? I like it here. Those children love me.'

'Shut the fuck up. To get out of here. Any ideas?'

'Ok, that way.'

'Which way?'

'That way.'

'Which way, you bum bell end.'

'There's no need for that camel dung, horseshit, fucker.'

'I'm going, ummmmmm, left.'

'You are very indecisive. Are you sure you don't want to stay.'

'Yes, only without you.'

'Well, that's not going to happen, now is it?'

'Just dreaming. Now forwards and onwards.'

They walked the walk and jumped the potholes. It was miles until they came across a town, hiding from any humans that wanted potential food or even a pet for their amusements. This was difficult because the more they walked, the more people were about. There were bikes everywhere and the smell of food at every corner.

Hedgy could smell fish and followed his nose. Eventually, he got lucky and came across a small backless lorry full of the stuff. There were mainly sharks that had no fins due to them being amputated whilst the fish were still alive. These had died due to firstly torture of their fins being ripped from their sides and then a slow death of oxygen-induced terror. Hedgy skidded on the wet floor and ended up in one of the plastic containers that were ready to be taken on board one of the whale catcher vessels.

One of the seamen from the Whalers picked up the container with Jeff and Hedgy in it and put it in the back of a truck. Then drove it to the ship ready to sail, loaded it on board and left. A few minutes later the ships engine churned the water and manoeuvred out of the dock.

'Hedgy, you've done it again.'

'Look, I slipped. It wasn't my fault.'

'It's always your fault.'

'Why? Just because I slipped?'

'No, because you don't watch where you're bloody going.'

'Stop picking on me. I'm fragile and very hungry.'

'You're always hungry.'

'So?'

Jeff and Hedgy perused their immediate domain. They could smell rotting fish and stale water. A man with a hosepipe sprayed the decking and splashed them with water. Jeff's Samurai paint make-up had run and Hedgy was covered in white paint with greyish black streaks. They also blended in with the fish colour they were lying with.

Hedgy manoeuvred enough to slip them over the side of the plastic container. They were in the big holding areas of the ship. It was dark and filled with activity. Men cleaning and preparing for their catch were busy.

Jeff looked at all four steel walls and Hedgy gasped at the vertical stairs.

'Jeff, how the hell are we going to climb those stairs? They're fit for snakes and insects to climb, not hangers on like us. Any ideas?'

Jeff in deep thought, looked around and then some. He studied what people were doing.

'Hedgy, you see that rope?'

'What rope?'

'That rope that's just about to hit you in the face.'

'Oouuuuch.'

'Ooooooops, too late.'

'Why didn't you tell me sooner? That bloody hurt.'

'Cos I only just saw it coming myself, dummy. Anyway, I was saying, you know that rope?'

'Ummm, yep.'

'If I twist myself around it, hold us on, and not let go? It should take us out of here.'

'Ok, sounds dangerous, why not give it a go?'

'Ok, here comes the rope again.'

'I'm not going anywhere, only with you, stupid.'

Jeff twisted his shaft as he described and the rope lifted. They swung to the top of the ship and were hauled to the decking, where they were spun into dizziness on descending. Jeff was so disoriented he let go, confused as to where he was.

Dumf, sting, splash. They both hit the water sideways. Salty seawater at that. Hedgy took a deep breath before entering but still came up coughing and spluttering.

Jeff sank upside down. Only Hedgy was buoyant and he splashed his little legs like mad to keep them alive. Jeff felt a push on his shaft and saw a huge eye looking straight at him.

'Hedgy, Hedgy, what the fuck. Get us out of here, fast. Turn left, no right. Monsters, we're going to be eaten alive.'

'I'm trying, I'm trying.'

'Faster, faster, faster.'

Jeff was hurled in the air and Hedgy's legs were like plastercine sticks, all over the place and jerked in all directions. A dolphin had found them and decided to use them as a plaything.

The dolphin left them to fall, just long enough to splash back into the sea. Then, with its nose, pushed either Jeff or Hedgy for another flight of fancy. Hedgy landed on the dorsal fin and held on for his life. The dolphin dived and Hedgy knew it. Hedgy was on the brink of running out of air when the dolphin raised its game to the surface, just in time. Hedgy did not let go for fear of something else happening. Hedgy, again went under with Jeff but lost his grip. The force of the dolphin's speed made it impossible to grip anymore. Another dolphin whisked them up into the air and both came down with a thud. They had landed in a Greenpeace vessel that was harassing the whaler's ship. Jeff heard shouting from the protesters. None had noticed Jeff and Hedgy's arrival. Ropes were thrown and ladders attached to the ship for the protesters to get on board. Some climbed and some people fell in the sea.

'What the hell are they doing?'

'Looks like they're angry at the whalers.'

'Hedgy, watch out.'

Crash! The ladders were pushed from the ship. It pinned Jeff and Hedgy into the corner of the boat. The Greenpeace people were trying to rescue their partners in pursuit, or saving the horrific deaths from the whalers and putting themselves in danger at the same time. As valiant the cause and noble for their attempt, they got nothing, only publicity. That in itself was amazing. The ladder was dismantled, people rescued and finally ropes, either kept or thrown back. The Greenpeace protesters decided to call it a day. They were exhausted. All that time in the same boat and nobody noticed the alien invasion, namely, Jeff and Hedgy travelling with them.

The skipper and his passengers were all native to Australia.

'How the hell did the Aussies get here?'

'Well, I don't know. Possibly swam.'

'Yes Hedgy, swam right. Swam from Oz? Like millions of miles away, swam, huh?'

'What planet are you on, Pal?'

'It's all a load of bollocks and bollocks to it all.'

'What you talking about?'

'Well, if you ask me, if we were going to die, we would have been dead by now.'

'And how D'you work that one out?'

'Because, we are still here, pal.'

'And ask yourself why, pal.'

'Why, what D'you mean?'

'My bollocks are still here and so am I, pal.'

'And...?'

'That means I'm immortal.'

'No it doesn't. It means you are fucking lucky.'

'You got it. That means I'm still alive and kicking and lucky with it ha, ha, ha.'

'Why are you always in trouble, Jeff? Is it because your gob works before your brain does?'

It took ages to get back to dry land. Darkness was upon them and eyes from every crevice, Hidey wholes, nooks, and crannies, were upon them all. Rats scurried, mice shuffled along the rocks, cats and dogs were on the alert for food. Everybody carried some kind of equipment with them. Unbeknown to the protesters, Jeff and Hedgy had dived into the nearest haversack. They were being carried to a Hotel room, which was on the fifth floor.

Hedgy and Jeff stayed still all night and rested after their extra ordinary day. They were awake earlier than expected with a bang, thud, and a pain in their sides. The haversack had been thrown on the floor and left.

'Not again, can't anybody get a good night's kip without being disturbed. Have they no understanding of thoughtfulness, for god sake.'

'That hurt. You all right, Jeff?'

'Well yes, I suppose so. Just tired, exhausted, and going back to sleep.'

'You can't. We have to move or be trod on. Now get your arse together and shimmy.'

'Shimmy, what's shimmy?'

'Just move will you.'

'Right we're off.'

Hedgy found the entrance to the haversack, looked out to see the coast was clear, and yet again, legged it. The hotel door to the room opened and Hedgy ran for his life. A man spotted them at the corner of his eye and gasped, 'What in blazes was that. Caron, you got rats?'

'Nah mate just a cat possibly.'

'Anyways cobber, I've cam ta see if you're ready to go home to Ozzy land of the wallaby.'

'Yeah, fair dinkum. I'm ready for me kangaroo pouch to rest in mate.'

'Shall I grab this suitcase and take it to the lobby?'

'Yeah, that would be good to go.'

Hedgy and Jeff as usual had a very narrow escape but were no nearer to home. They managed to get into the empty lift all the way down to ground floor, outside and onto the beach over the road from the Hotel.

It was a pebbled beach, rough and ready, and full of rubbish. Hedgy sat and admired all the debris.

'Hey, hey you?'

'Who us?'

'Yes you. Git off my beach.'

'Your beach?'

'Yes, my beach. Clear off.'

'No.'

'Clear off or I'll bite you.'

'And I'll bite back.'

'I will, I'm warning you. Go on chufta, chufta.

'What does that mean?'

'It means chufta off now. And stay away.'

Hedgy stood on a piece of old wood, which was about three by three foot in diameter.

'What's your name?'

'Why?'

'Because I want to know.'

'What for?'

'Look clear off. I'm not looking for friends. They call me Sammy No Nutts, why?'

'Sammy No, what?'

'Look and listen, Sammy No Nutts.'

With that in mind he lifted one of his back legs and revealed he really did not have any bollocks, hence the phrase 'SAMMY NO NUTTS'.

Jeff started laughing and Hedgy too. Sammy no nutts was getting agitated and prancing up and down with an anxious strut.

'Go on. Go and strut your stuff on somebody else's beach. This one's mine. Shove off, will ya?'

'No, we want to stay here for a bit.'

'For a bit of what, exactly?'

'For a bit of peace and quiet, so shut the fuck up.'

'Chufta, chufta, chufta nuts. Get off my beach, Nooowwwwww.'

'Nooooooo.'

Sammy No Nutts was a corgi style, Alsatian look alike. His legs were firm and stubby. He had a wonderful, full of mischief face, and an optimistic charismatic attitude with ambience. He was certainly a loud, bubbly, character. A no nonsense, kind of woofy that people were aware of.

He shouted at two cats just about to step on his beach, 'hey, hey, sling your hook.' Chufta, chufta off.'

The cats hissed and screeched at him and went on their way, away from the beach. Meanwhile back at the wood that Hedgy was standing on started to move. Sammy No Nutts stood on it and it started to drift out to sea.

'Hey No Nutts Sammy, what did you do that for?'

'My beach, you chufta off.'

The wood drifted further and further until it hit the waves and then went faster out to see.

'Hey chufta Nutts, help us get back and we will get off your beach.'

'Nah, you should have thought of that earlier. And my name is not chufta Nutts, its Sammy. Bye and don't come back.'

'You're horrid, you are. Fancy forcing us away like that. Horrid is what you are and horrid you will stay.'

The beach became a distant memory, and the sea vast and deep. The driftwood dipped according to which wave hit what part. Hedgy stayed in the middle, hoping that the balance would not knock them over board. It worked. They were balancing the board with the elements for days. They drifted for miles and tasted rain, many times.

'I need a drink. Water, water everywhere and not a drop to drink.'

'If anybody can hear us, we need food, water, a bed, Jacuzzi and a slide.'

'What, you stupid. Why a Jacuzzi and a slide.'

'Why not this place is boring. All you can see is blue with a twinge of white bubbles riding the waves. It's ridiculously boring. Bring on watching paint dry for a change.'

'Hey, did you see that?'

'Huh, what?'

'There it is again.'

'No nothing. Hallucinating, are we. You know what seawater does to the brain, don't you.'

'Well it would cure your dysfunctional grey matter then, won't it?'

'Oohh listen to youuuuuuu.'

'Oi stop that.'

'Stop what I have not moved from your big behind, Hedgy.'

'Oohh, there it goes again.'

'What goes where again?'

'That. Now you felt that because it nearly knocked us into the water.'

'Uummmm, maybe. Ok what was it? A huge boulder, no doubt. A rock of ages sticking out the water.'

'Well, considering the sea could be hundreds of miles down by now, I don't think it was anything to do with land, pal.'

'Maybe a whale swimming alongside us?'

At that point, a long dolphin nose appeared out of nowhere and nudged the wood. It was a tiny nose and its length told them it was a baby dolphin. It must have been curious as to what the driftwood was all about. Next came big, huge Mamma and Jeff noticed her straight away. It was the one that rescued them when they were in trouble with the Greenpeace movement sometime last week.

'It's the dolphin that saved us.'

'And how D'you know that then?'

'Because if you look at the tip of her nose she has an old wound that is lighter than her normal nose colour. Seeeeeee.'

'Well, you amaze me. You really are alert sometimes, Jeff. Give the prick a blue badge for observational gallantry.'

'Stop taking the piss. And that reminds me.'

'You dare, you just dare. Piss backwards if you must, but don't you dare piss on me.'

'Oohh, ooo, arrrh too late.'

Hedgy looked to see a fountain of yellow stuff but nothing.

'Only joking, my friend. Ha, ha, ha.'

Weeing in the sea was their only option and the dolphins swam a safe distance because they did not want to be urinated on either. After a couple of minutes or so Mamma came back and baby swam the other side of the wood. Mamma pushed the wood into super speed mode for miles. And then baby took over for a few kilometres. In the distance, all saw something jumping out of the water. It looked to be tiny fish but a school of them. The dolphins stopped what they were doing and swam towards their food time.

Sharks fins arrived on the scene and their fins were huge, bigger than the dolphins. Baby dolphin swam back to them and dropped a tiny fish on top of the wood.

'Arh, bless its little cotton socks, food. It's given us food.'

The baby dolphin swam off again to find Mamma. It came back a few minutes later with another tiny fish and did the same. It kept doing it until Hedgy was covered in these fish. Not only that, these poor fish were flapping and wriggling for their life. Hedgy started to put them back into the sea without baby watching. Eventually under the mound was a dead one. Hedgy ripped it apart and chewed like no tomorrow. He was over hungry, devoured every bit of flesh, and let the bones drop in the sea of replenishment. He also managed to prize the bones out of his tiny teeth. Shark fins encircled the driftwood. Jeff was eager to stay in the middle of the solid floor. Hedgy saw them too and gripped onto anything solid. When the wood moved via waves so did they. Mamma dolphin suddenly saw what was going on and with baby dolphin gave chase but she was out numbered. Not only that, baby was in danger. Suddenly there were dolphins everywhere chasing each shark fin that could be seen in the water. The dolphins were playing shark chase and tantalizing jumping challenges. They revelled in trying to make the sharks scared and angry. Finally, the sharks could see they were so far out of their depth and comfort zone. They swam away as quick as they came. Baby dolphin looked up and swam gently passed to make sure its newfound friends were safe. Mamma dolphin tipped the wood and carried on pushing to other parts of the water. Some other dolphins took over and in a few days, they actually saw the tips of land. Jeff and Hedgy were so excited, when they jumped for joy they fell off the driftwood. Baby managed to throw them back on again and the journey carried on.

Jeff felt his body drying up. He had been on the driftwood for nearly a couple of weeks. Luckily, for their friends, they were kept alive by their generosity, care, and understanding. Their lives were put in dolphin fins hands, and survived.

TIE ME KANGAROO DOWN POUCH

The tide was coming in and the driftwood too. Hedgy stepped off the floor and fell head first into the water. He did not gauge the depth and thought it was much shallower than it looked. He came up coughing and spluttering in his usual way. Jeff just loved the coolness of his shaft and dragged through sand while Hedgy got his sea legs swimming upside down as usual. They had touched down and Hedgy managed to get completely on land with no water between them. They laid there in the baking sun just so relieved to be on firm ground again. Again, they did not know where they were but it was not familiar ground nor safe.

Hedgy scurried to some shade and out of site. Night came early and Jeff woke to the sound of shuffling. That sound was quickly coming their way. Hedgy saw what looked like upside down dark plates coming for them. Hedgy dived into a hole only to find a green turtle trying to dig into it. She had both paws, fins, feet, in the sand and pushed the sand away to get deeper and deeper. The only problem with that was, every time she dug deeper, Hedgy and Jeff fell and fell. She then turned around and squirted white eggs at them, walked forward and shovelled the sand over the eggs, Jeff, and Hedgy. Hedgy and Jeff got sand in their eyes and as well as the dark could see nothing. Luckily for them, there was an opening so that they could just about breathe.

Jeff and Hedgy stayed put all night and when they woke up to the sunshine glaring at them with full on heat, they gently stepped through the very soft eggs until they reached the top of the hole. The last egg carefully trudged around and their first full on step after the climb out of the hole was a relief to say the least. Hedgy walked inland and found a fresh water stream. They drank so much; Hedgy thought his belly would sink into the river. Jeff bathed his shaft and noticed he was flaking bits of skin.

'You're flaking and falling to bits, you are.'

'What D'you mean?'

'You must have caught the sun on the driftwood and now you are skinning.'

'What's skinning.'

'Honestly, I have to explain everything to you. You really are a...'

Another rustle in the undergrowth, but this time it was far too near for comfort. Jeff was over alert and looked all over. Hedgy crouched down to hide so that he could not be seen. Whatever it was, it passed as quick as it came. They were still basking in the stream.

After a very long soak, both were very refreshed and back to near normal. Hedgy climbed and briskly walked through the undergrowth, practically all day. At night, they slept under boulder, bush, or hidey-hole. They were in Cape Hills National Park, Queensland, Australia.

A jumping thingy landed in front of them and then as quickly as it came as quick as it went. Later another thingy jumped and missed them by inches. Then another but this time it stopped in front of them, rather abruptly. It turned and Jeff said, 'jump in its bag or it will squash us.'

Hedgy did not have time to think. He just did as he was told. In the bag, they flew and met a very tiny creature that only looked to be a very new baby kangaroo. It was sucking on a nipple until it had company, then it let go and coward into a corner.

'What did you tell me to come in here for? Can't you see it's already occupied?'

'Hi little fella. Don't be afraid of Hedgy. He's not all that bad, just very grumpy at present.'

'How we going to get out of this one then, clever dip shit?'

'Well, we will have to fly or swim, or float or glide, or just climb and walk, stupid.'

'You are totally insane. You know that don't you?'

'And who's been telling you lies, then? You know nothing.'

'I know we're going to have to stick our bums out to have a shit because we can't do it here.'

'Well I'm all right Jack because I can just piss where I want to.'

'Please not on the baby and certainly not on me.'

'Well, shut the fuck up, then.'

Ten minutes of shear bliss. There was no arguing, no shouting, and not a confrontation in site. Baby kangaroo started to suckle again and this time without disturbance. Kangaroo Mom rested down for the night and when morning came, she hopped around smoothly. Her pouch was so big that Jeff could not see over the top to find where they were hopping too.

Hedgy felt two nipples that were not being used and so, to his delight, latched on. Mother kangaroo felt his bite and wriggled to acknowledge her discomfort. With a little adjusting and gentleness, Hedgy was able to stay on the teat and suckle. He found it a very pleasant experience and brought back such happy memories. Kangaroo Mom hopped for miles inland and rested for the night.

'Hedgy, you stink. You stink of a fanny that hasn't been washed in a month.'

'What D'you mean, a fanny.'

'Well put it this way, you need a virginal scrub kit, mate.'

'No I don't.'

'Oh yes you do. If, tie me Kangaroo down, Mom smells your fish she will throw us both out. Cover yourself in milk or something.'

'Don't be stupid.'

'I mean it, you Ming, hummmmm, and pong.'

'Well I can't smell anything.'

'You know what they say; a dog can't smell its own shit. Well this is fish at its absolute worst.'

'Well how come the little fella down here has not noticed?'

'Well, maybe he is being polite, pal.'

The Mother kangaroo stuck her head in the pouch and sniffed odorous fish fanny disgust and got hold of Jeff's shaft and threw them out onto the dirt track she was running on.

Dummffff, they hit the deck. Rolling time and time again, they gambolled into a bush and startled they found new company. A rattlesnake with the biggest rattle they had ever come across.

'There, there fella, no biting now. We come in peace.'

'There, there snake we are not your enemy. No biting now and stop that awful hissing.'

'Snaky, just leave us alone and we will be out of here before you can say kangarooooooooooooo.'

Hedgy quickly found his feet and legged it, just as the snake was about to pounce and bite with forked tongue.

'Phew, that was too close for my liking.'

'I'm fed up with this every time we land somewhere there's danger.'

'Come on there's a pub up ahead. Your favourite, Jeff.'

'Woo hoooo. Things are looking up at last. That was lucky.'

They chased the memory of Germany's finest beer only to find the place packed with Aussie, loud mouths. They were all holding some kind of beverage and gulped as fast as they could. The noise level was loud, rowdy, and jolly.

Hedgy stepped over the doorway and was swooped by an Aussie bloke onto the bar where they were encouraged to entertain the locals by dancing or singing, in fact anything that could be acknowledged as entertainment. The blokes were so pissed they were at that stage they would've laughed at anything moving.

Hedgy started to sing, 'frigin in the rigin, frigin in the rigin, frigin in the rigin cos there's fuck all else to do.'

He just sang it over and over again for about an hour then changed to, 'I wanna git out of this place, cos it's the last place I wanna be, I wanna git out of this place, cos there's a better place for you and me.'

That went on for another hour. The barmaid gave them a small, low dish of local beer, which helped with their vocal cords.

Another rendition of, 'surfing U.S.A. and how much is that doggy in the window was found to be a favourite. Overall, a good night was had by all. Others were so drunk they chose to not remember and some even slept with the snakes. Jeff and Hedgy were left to fend for themselves. They ended up under one of the seats situated around the room. Hedgy snored so sweetly. A snore of complete and utter calmness and a little bit of relaxation in the tones. Jeff was slumped over and his bell end touched the floor. He was over relaxed and his shaft only slightly moved with the blowing of Hedgy's snoring ability.

Late that morning, the barmaid came down to open up. Hedgy grunted and saw some crisps and nuts that had been spilt on the floor. Before the cleaners came in, Hedgy dashed over and vacuumed the lot up. He did not even take a breath. Then, he moved over to the next culinary corner of delights. It was again only crisps but it was sustenance all the same. He also loved his junk food, hamburgers being his favourite of all his delights.

Hedgy's excuse also, was to eat as much as he could get his paws on because he was eating for two, himself, and Jeff. Jeff had no mouth and only communicated through thought to Hedgy. He could see but with having no mouth, Hedgy ate for both of them. That gave Hedgy great delight. Some foods Jeff loved and others he loathed. Either way Hedgy had the upper hand. In addition, Hedgy monopolised what, when and where he could find food. He was an opportunist and lived for food.

As he sniffed through the pub floor, he came across a weird looking object and climbed into it. After he got in, they could not get out. They were stuck like glue in this metal tube thing.

Night-time came and the crowd of locals came in gangs to celebrate another knees up. No women, only men were there. Hedgy screeched and one of the Aussie blokes picked them up. He blew through the metal thing and found no noise coming from it. He looked inside and there was an almighty rush of laughter, which filled the pub room. With a little tug and manipulation, Jeff and Hedgy came out by force. The locals were still laughing and the Aussie bloke started to blow his instrument that Jeff and Hedgy had got stuck in. The night was young and the melodies flowed. All night singing was on the menu and Hedgy engaged in all that happiness all over again. This time they tried to sing songs from the band QUEEN. It did not sound too accurate but who was marking them for perfection.

The next morning was the same as the first but this time Jeff had a hangover and wanted nothing more than to be left alone. Hedgy on the other hand was eager to go, find food, explore, and see the sites more.

'Keep still will you. My head feels loose.'

'Come on I want to find food outside maybe.'

'Just stay and stop fidgeting, will you.'

'Me fidget.'

'Shhhhhhhh.'

'I am not staying in this pub one more minute, so get yourself together. We're off.'

'Get myself, what?'

'Together, pal. We're going to explore Aussie land.'

'Just give us half a day to, get myself together, you say?'

'No, we're off now. So, pull yourself together.'

'Nobody can pull themselves together. It's a fallacy, stupid.'

'Oohh but you can.'

'And how D'you do that then?'

'Wellllll, I don't know. It's just a saying, isn't it? It means change the way you are and get ready to be normal.'

'That is such a stupid saying. Nobody can actually pull themselves together, because they are already together. Also pull, pull what. Metaphor for what?'

'I don't know. Look, just let's go.'

'No, I have not yet pulled myself, as you call it together yet. It could take a couple of months, years, decades at this rate. What a stupid saying.'

'All right, you've made your point. Can we just move now?'

'Please just spend some time pulling yourself apart because I am not going anywhere.'

Hedgy was just about to move, 'And if you move, I will piss on you, seriously.'

'Now that's black mail, pal.'

'Just give me a couple of hours sleep then.'

'Oohh all right then, but you better make it quick.'

'A couple of hours quick and don't wake me. I want to wake myself up, thank you.'

Hedgy fell on his legs deliberately and stretched for Jeff's convenience. They both fell asleep and Jeff woke up gently, quietly and noticed his little friend snoring. He smiled and let him snore to his heart's content. Jeff just thought about all the things they had been through and where they had ended up. It was an incredible journey. A journey that not many creatures could have achieved, yet they had done so much in so little time and still there to tell the tale. Wow, what an achievement.

It ended up being a tranquil, slow moving day with lots of catching up to do. Hedgy woke up gently yawning his head off and totally relaxed.

'Have you pulled yourself together yet, Hedgy?'

'Ummm yes, I think so. It is a stupid saying, isn't it Jeff.'

'Well, I was trying to tell you. It means nothing to anything and when you think about it, it's an impossible task for any living thing.'

'Uuummmm, did you sleep well?'

'Very well, thanks.'

'I think it's time we left because if we stay we will be in danger of becoming drunkards.'

'Well, after today my head says leave and my body wants to dance the fandango. That means I need to get out of here and save my yearning for another pub local focal, vocal, local.'

'You really are mad, Jeffrey.'

'Don't call me Jeffrey. Only my Mom called me Jeffrey. And that was when she was angry with me.'

'Wow, you remembered a little about your past.'

'Yes, and it wasn't very nice, pal.'

'Come on lets mosey along to another corral.'

The terrain was flat as far as the eye could see. Dry shrubbery and the prospect of slithering snakes under every available bush. Skulls of dead goats and the occasional kangaroo skeleton were prevalent. They saw in the corner of their eyes the scurrying of scorpions, mice, and insects. There was no water to be seen or even sniffed at in any direction. There was the occasional succulent but the taste was bitter and almost unpalatable. Hedgy did try a number of times but spat it out. He also wondered whether some were poisonous.

They walked forever, again in the baking sun and were running out of life when an aboriginal man came to their rescue. Hedgy was limp and Jeff limper.

The man looked them over carefully bemused, then laughed, and then passed them over to his brother who had just come out of a bush with loads of large white grubby worms in his hand. They exchanged what they had in their hands and the other man just shook his head in not understanding what he was looking at. Hedgy hissed at him and he dropped him on the ground. Hedgy was ready to leg it but the other man managed to grab Hedgy's back leg and then grab hold of the rest of his body. He said something in aboriginal to the brother and they exchanged again. This time the brother laughed and more words were exchanged. Jeff was squeezed and prodded.

'Dingo dick, huh,'the brother said in an Aussie accent.

The other brother laughed aloud and a crowd of aboriginal men and women encircled the brother holding Jeff and Hedgy.

'I think we're going to be famous again, Hedgy.'

'I don't want to be famous. I just want to be put down and left to me own devices, thank you.'

'Anybody want my autograph, then.'

'They want to know what you're about, Jeff. Just tell them you're one big dick and they'll all go home.'

'You're nasty, you are.'

'No I'm not. You are.'

'And how D'you work that one out?'

'You got attached to me remember and given me grief ever since, pal.'

'I thought you wanted, needed, and loved me. I thought you couldn't live without me. I thought wrong didn't I, my bestist friend ever in the whole wide world.'

'Get real. You are only here for the ride, pal.'

'I know you love me because you told me in your sleep, this afternoon. You dreamt out loud, Jeff don't leave me, you're my friend, I need you. You mean the world to me.'

'Yeah, right.'

'You are a great big Rasta blaster, liar, pal.'

'No, not me sexy Hedgy, kitty, kitty.'

'I am not a kitten, you stupid dip stick, fuck whit.'

'Well stop sounding like you are meeeooowwwing about nothing then, will you?'

'Rasta blaster liar. You're bums on fire. Rasta blaster, liar. You're dicks on fire. Rasta blaster liar, home is where the fart is. And you're one big fart so spread the word and go, pal.'

'As I was saying, you're very, very, very, very nasty, you are'

The whole aboriginal gang walked for miles and then some. They eventually reached a corrugated house, which was their home. It was a village of huts, mud huts, timber huts, and fences for their animals. It had a kind of formation about it. Some organization in its structures. The land was bone dry and looked to be a very hard life to live. They are people that take advantage of their whole nature and surroundings. They share the land with their inhabitants.

The man holding them tied them up outside his house and gave Hedgy some huge caterpillars to eat, known as witchety grubs. Hedgy thought he had eaten worse, so he tucked in. It wriggled a little and then died. Hedgy found it quite nice and was given another one. After that, another but was left to eat alone.

'Honestly, you eat anything.'

'Yes, and it keeps both you and me alive, stupid.'

'I know but do you have to chew on huge bugs. Can't you eat some kind of meat, egg, or cheese?'

'Yes, I will just ask him shall I? Does he speak hedgehog, then?'

'Ask him, stupid.'

'You ask him, if you're so clever. You ask for two steak and chips and side salad for your evening meal, pal.'

'Ok, point taken. I will shut up shall I?'

'Chomp, chomp, sounds good.'

Hedgy finished his last bite. The head was crunched between his teeth and swallowed nearly whole. He managed to get it down all the same.

'I could do with a drink of water. Can you see any?'

Jeff was looking around and did not hear Hedgy's request.'

'Hey, hey water. I need water.'

'Yes and I need for you to stop pestering me and demanding.'

'Just water will do. Can you see any?'

'Ummmmm, over there. Over by the donkey goat.'

'What? Donkey goat. You surely mean one or the other don't you.'

'Well you look what would you call it?'

Hedgy analysed the thing and realised it was a baby donkey that was covered in mud and tied to a stake in the ground.'

'Arh Jeff, it's a baby ass. Just like you, cos you're an ass. Ha, ha, ha.'

'Do you want water or don't you?'

'Yes please.'

'Well, you will have to go over there and we are tied up here and here is too far from there.'

'So we will have to get over there somehow, won't we?'

'Go on then.'

Hedgy tugged on the rope and Jeff jerked his way, but nothing happened. Hedgy chewed all the way through the rope and it snapped. They ran to where the water was and drank. The baby donkey went over and drank with them.

'Hi ya, ware da you cam from?'

'From over there.'

He was an Aussie sassy assie and was nosy to talk to someone different for a change.

'Hi Chuck, Chick, Chuckle, Chattle, Chortle, and Mish Mash.'

'Wow, that was a family mouthful. How do you remember all the ducklings names like that?'

'Well, its easy really. They all begin with a ch, except the twins; cos Mish and Mash are from another mother who sadly drowned when a boat ran over her.'

'Oh, that's terrible. Why only two?'

'Well, that's all the baby's she had.'

'Come on you wanna bee's, move your ass and give space to my brood. Come in through. Chortle, keep up will ya?'

'You'd better move cos she has a sharp beak and she ain't afraid to use it.'

Hedgy quickly shuffled to one side and Jeff was chuffed at how cute they all looked, waddling along after each other. One by one, all in line, they waddled into the water. Mother watched the parade and would not move until Mish and Mash being the last, were comfortably floating in a group, waiting for they're Mamma to join them. Once in, the family floated according to fitness, ability and speed. That meant as per usual, Mish and Mash were last.

An aboriginal man came out and realised that Jeff and Hedgy were loose. He had something in his hand and threw it at them.

'Ruuuuunnnnn, it's a boomerang. He's thrown his boomerang. If it hits you, you're a gonna, for sure.'

Hedgy tried to duck but Jeff just froze. They saw a beautifully decorated piece of half moon shaped wood. Only it was the same width wise and curved to enhance hitting power to the victim intended. The idea was to throw it at a moving target to stop it in its tracks, dead. They did not know whether it was thrown wrongly or badly made, but this boomerang hit Jeff's bollocks, spun him around and Hedgy into the air, twirled then around again in dizziness and Hedgy grabbed onto a metal bar that was in front of him. It turned out to be one of those silent, wind elevated, one-man planes. Hedgy grabbed hold of the wheel bar and Jeff twisted his shaft around the side metal wheel bar. They hung on as if it were a near death experience.

A man sitting in his trike Buggy Nano Delta, one-man plane, had just taken off. Jeff and Hedgy were so lucky to be able to latch onto his fuselage, just in the nick of time.

Hedgy had no way of getting comfortable or changing his paws for comfort. Jeff gripped so tight that he could feel blood warm up and his bell end became malleable. They hung on, it seemed for hours. Jeff realised they were coming out of the clouds. They landed in Indonesia, refuelled, and took off again straight away. Jeff and Hedgy managed to get a firmer grip and stop the cramps in Hedgy's legs. They took off straight away with other hang glider companions. It looked to be a regular 14 as the men driving were very familiar with his route and spoke nice and friendly to his other hang glider buddies.

Again, Jeff and Hedgy just clung onto their passage and eventually reached Kazakhstan. It actually landed in the middle of the country in a wasteland of shrubbery and dry dirt areas. It did not look as if much grew or lived there.

Hedgy, by this time, was exhausted, stiff and just let go of his destiny when they touched down. Jeff limped over and both flopped to the ground. After a few minutes to recoup, Hedgy loosened his stiff torso to a bush not far from whence they literally dropped off at. Jeff saw the pilot of their vehicle dismantle the plane and put it into a huge lorry.

'More bruises than the last time. I always, always land arse over tit and come out worse.'

'How are we going to get off this one?'

'I don't honestly know. There's know where to go. It is a dessert and a forest. Which part is best for us, Jeff?'

'Just find us somewhere safe to hide.'

'Look Jeff, look over there.'

'Where?'

'There, that multi-coloured balloon thing. There.'

'What, where, over bloody where?'

'Over bloody there, where them men are.'

'Can't you hear them?'

'Arh yes, over that way, there. Why didn't you say?'

'I did.'

'What is it? It has some kind of square basket attached to it.'

'It's a hot air balloon.'

'What's the basket for?'

'It's a hot air balloon.'

'What's the balloon for?'

'It's a hot air balloon.'

'It can't be theirs, cos there's no hot air. That's stupid.'

'You blithering idiot. The machine in the middle blows hot air out, so the hot air lifts the balloon material to create the lift.'

'What machine. I can't see no bloody machine. What you talking about, woman?'

'Why do I even listen to you? You know nothing, and don't call me a woman. Just call me by my proper name, Hedgy.'

'I know your name but you act just like a woman, nag, bloody nag, nag, nag.'

'Right, we're off.'

With that, Hedgy stretched his legs and raced towards the balloon. Without the authority of Jeff the me, me; telling Hedgy what to do. They clambered up the rope and hid under the sand bags that were tied to the inside of the basket. About five or six loud roaring bellows came from up above and you could visibly see flames being thrown into the middle of the balloon. It was warm where Jeff and Hedgy were but not intense. One man got in, then managed the heat control and another gave orders. Another man rushed around on the ground outside to untie the balloon from the ground pegs. The balloon lifted high. The controller made the fire roar even more and then stop in spurts every few minutes or so. He kept doing this until they were at their particular level of height. Hedgy and Jeff were careful not to make a sound, nor move.

'Do you think they saw us?'

'No.'

'Do you think they heard us?'

'Jeff?'

'What?'

'Shut the fuck up. SLEEP!'

'I don't want to sleep.'

'All right then, just shut the fuck up, then.'

Jeff fell asleep and Hedgy kept watch. He was excited. He had never been up in one of these balloons before and found it fascinating. The rainbow colours of the balloon were mesmerising.

Jeff woke up freezing. Hedgy's breath was smoking where hot and cold air met each other. The two men in the basket had heavy thick coats on.

'Why is it so cold? Where are we?'

'How the hell do I know? It's bloody cold though.'

The hot air balloon had reached the edge of Sweden and was preparing to descend onto land below. There were so many trees covered in fluffy white snow. It was difficult to find land to fall onto.

LIGHTS, CAMERA, ACTION

The air was cleaner than clean and rushed to everyone's lungs. You could almost taste the freshness of Sweden as they bumped onto fresh, crisp, whiter than white snow. It was a snow like no other. The snow heightened the brilliance of the sun glare. To touch was like crystal powder that melted in an instant. The day was surprisingly warm considering.

The basket crunched to a halt and the balloon swayed back and forth, until it deflated and limply, flopped to one side of the basket. The men got out and started to squash the balloon down by pulling on its ropes and drawing it in. This was not an easy task. By the time the men had finished, they were mentally and physically exhausted. Just for a giggle one of the men lay in the snow on his back, pushed, and pulled his arms and legs out and in. He then got up and in the snow was a shape of an angel, wearing a long dress silhouetted with wings. Both men were ecstatic. At the same time, Hedgy climbed out of the basket, dropped into the snow like a heavy brick, and disappeared. Quick thinking Hedgy grabbed hold of the dangling rope. A truck pulled up beside the basket and missed Hedgy by inches.

'That was bloody close. He nearly had my legs squashed.'

'You're lucky, his wheel arch nearly lopped my taja in half.'

The balloon, basket, men, Hedgy and Jeff were negotiated onto the back or into the truck. There was an overwhelming amount of camera equipment that had been on board the craft. They had taken professional cameras with them. The countryside had a weird, freshness about it and you could see obvious wildlife close by watching your every move, yet far enough away to be safe from predators.

'We're being watched. Even the trees have eyes. Look, a twinkle sparkle.' There coming for us.'

'Don't be stupid, Jeff. Calm down. Oh, I saw another one.'

'What is it? I mean, what are they?'

'Uummmm, I dunno. They've got ruddy great big horny antlers and a huge snout though.'

The sunshine was intense and jumped off every glistening article, moving or otherwise. Jeff and Hedgy felt rather warm. By the time they got to the unplanned destination, the men had taken their heavy coats off and just had thin polo neck tee shirts, with jeans on but their boots were definitely made for trudging through deep snow.

They arrived at a large warehouse, where they unloaded their stuff. Jeff and Hedgy were still not spotted and became part of the furniture.

A woman came by and was wolf whistled by two of the men. The woman grinned cheekily and noticed Jeff hanging on for dear life from the rope attached to the balloon basket rope. She told the man to stop a minute, while she untangled Jeff and Hedgy.

'Oi, oi.'

'Oi, oi, get off. Leave us alone. Oi.'

The woman smiled and said in Swedish, "ha, ha, det är en dildo."('ha, ha, it's a Dildo.')

"Vad är? Vad pratar du om? "('What is? What are you talking about?')

She held Jeff and Hedgy up, then replied, "Det här! Vi skulle kunna använda detta I vår nya film. "('This! We could use this in our new film.')

The man looked closer as Hedgy hissed and said, "Det är en penis." ('It's a Penis.')

The woman laughed, then realised they were more intrigued than ever to see a real live thing that had a huge penis attached to its back.

"Jag ska visa Hantz. Vi hörs senare. "('I'm going to show Hantz. Talk to you later.')

"Inte hålla mig vänta för länge. Vi kunde flytta berg tillsammans, du och jag "('Don't keep me waiting too long. We could move mountains together, you and I.')

"Ok, vi kommer att flytta varandra senare, ja?"('Ok, we will move each other later, yes?')

"Ok, ja."('Ok, yes.')

She held Jeff and Hedgy at arms- length and carried them into the film studio. They were filming on set as they do so. A beautiful auburn, longhaired woman was in the middle of peeling off her jeans. Then came her scantily clad knickers. She bared all for the muscly man knelt behind her and then he gently penetrated her soft loveliness. She moaned and groaned. The man concentrated on his manly action and oozed passion, wrapped with self –indulgence.

Jeff could not take his eyes off the action.

'I can do that. Hey, it's my turn.'

'Jeff, stop shouting. They can't hear you. Anyway, they wouldn't want you doing anything like that.'

'But, I can do that. I can do that better than he can.'

The woman stood there watching until the scene was completed. She went to the Director and showed him Jeff and Hedgy. By this time, Hedgy decided to just wriggle. The director was amazed, excited and could not wait to have them in his new film as actors.

The woman was called Fran. She found a cardboard box for Jeff and Hedgy to sit in and took them to her dressing room. She put the box on her dressing table and stroked Jeff's shaft. Jeff was elated and wanted more but she needed to get ready for her performance with her newly found actors, namely Jeff and Hedgy.

After a while, they all waited for the show to begin. Jeff was washed and looked sensationally healthy, clean, and tidy for his prospective audience. Hedgy had been brushed and cleaned as well. They all waited and waited and waited.

The director called Fran over, said a few words in Swedish and she then came back excited with a shining grin. She grabbed hold of Jeff's shaft and walked on the set. It had a double bed with a floral duvet set and on the side a pretend bathroom. The bath was white, high on one side and taps in the middle of one side. The décor was painted a very light greyish, antique green walls and white woodwork. It reminded Jeff of home from home, of what he could remember and that was very little indeed. She laid on the bed with her knees up.

'Come on; let the dog see the rabbit.'

'You're disgusting.'

'No I'm not. I am sexually charged and am desperate for a bit of how's your father.'

'How's your father? What does that mean, how's your father, indeed?'

'Never mind. Come on girl. Get them, there knickers off. I'm ready.'

'Oh cripes, what next?'

'Come on, stop teasing. Dog, rabbit, dog, rabbit? For Christ's sake, get a move on.'

Jeff was almost overly excited. Suddenly he went in. Fanny, freckling all the way down pleasure down alley. He could feel the warmth of her orgasms and the rhythm of her sliding. She had obviously done this before. She moaned excessively. Jeff thought she must have been acting. He's good but not that bloody good. She started howling and wriggling and as quick as Jeff went in, as quickly, he was pulled out, dripping.

'Maybe I was that good all the time, then?'

'Maybe she's an actress and played up to the camera, then.'

'Maybe I liked my version better, thank you.'

'Please yourself.'

The director came over to Fran and muttered to her in Swedish. The camera man re-organised his lenses and after five minutes said, "ok Fran, göra det igen och tiden inte titta in I kameran. Du ska se naturligt. Det är inte en annons." ('ok Fran, do it again and this time don't look into the camera. You are supposed to look natural. It's not an advertisement.')

'What, not again. I can't go in again. I've done my bit.'

Hedgy roared with laughter. His sounds were heard all over the studio.

"Fran kan du lugna ner dem lite. Ge honom ett kex eller något. "('Fran can you calm them down a little. Give him a biscuit or something.')

Fran wiped Jeff down with a damp sponge and then towelled him dry. She then gave Hedgy one of the biscuits out of the tea break biscuit tins. Hedgy munched. Fran prepared herself and Jeff, yet again went in. Hedgy nearly choked on the crumbs. The cameraman could hear and see Hedgy choke. He called for everything to stop. Jeff was so engrossed in going in a second time; he was not going to stop. He was enjoying his rubbing and sexual, sensual feelings. He had not felt like this for a long, long time and felt privileged to be going in a second time.

'What, get off me? Leave me.'

'Cough, splutter, choke, heave. Cough, splutter, choke, heave, wretch. 'For god sake Hedgy, what a time to get a cold. You are ruining everything. Breath, just breath.'

'I cough, can't, cough, choke, heave.'

'I know you're a cunt, just breath.'

Another five minutes had gone. This time Jeff went in wondering what else was going to happen. His concentration had lapsed and he was borderline flopperdy, doo, dah.

In all, Jeff went in about five more times and his sex life took a turn for the worse. Shagging that many times was torturous.

They had been at it for hours. The director was a finicky fucker. Every minute part of the set had to be just so. The actions had to be precisely what he envisaged and the timing of each particular move had to be played out impeccably to his forethought. The director was a bullyboy with arrogance but his results were amazing. That was the reason why actors put up with such a man and that was because his results paid a high price to success.

At last, the director called time out for lunch. Jeff withered with exhaustion. Never had so much sexual pleasure been so badly abused, for so long and for such a cause.

Hedgy was given some carrots, mashed potato, and cabbage to chomp on. He really wanted a nice big juicy beef burger with relish and a tiny bit of salad for decoration. But no, he got organically grown, straight from the earth, veg fix. It was awful and he knew that this sort of food would not go well, plus play havoc with his ablutions. He needed water and plenty of it but instead she gave them a bowl of liquid soup from the boiled vegetables. Hedgy was in no mood to go healthy and kicked the boiled watered stew all over Fran's script.

He also just missed Fran's dressing gown as she darted away from the scene of the deliberate accident.

'Oi, I saw that.'

'You did?'

'Yes and you are acting like a spoilt child.'

'What of it?'

'What's wrong with it?'

'You try eating soul food with no real soul.'

'Soul food? It looked to me like food that had roots and healthy, feel good nosh.'

'No, it's more like unhealthy, to chew a lot of garbage, and the drink is piss water. You should try it.'

'Yes, very good Hedgy. You know I can't chew because I haven't got a mouth, stupid.'

'Well make one then. Just get a knife and slit your throat, why don't you?'

'I am not going down suicide alley. Not for you or anybody for that matter. You just keep chomping on the good life and I'll just keep sitting pretty for the both of us.'

'Yeah right, chuckle. You sit pretty. What a joke. You are the most ugliest looking prick I've ever seen.'

'And how many pricks have you seen, apart from yours, obviously?'

'Well, there's that one over there. Now that's a fine specimen. Then there's, uummmm that one over there. Now that's even better, over there.'

Jeff felt exhausted still and as he looked around at other penises that Hedgy was pointing out, his inferiority complex kicked in. 'Hedgy, shut the fuck up. What are you trying to do?' Make me feel small?'

'I don't need to. You can do that all by yourself, pal.'

Jeff's ego flew out of the window. His ambition diminished into oblivion.

Fran was told to be dressed and come back tomorrow. The director had made other arrangements on the spot and changed his working day around to accommodate his filming schedule. Jeff gladly went back in his box and Hedgy was ecstatic about being pulled away from his fabulously healthy, crappy lunch.

It was cold outside and Fran put Jeff and Hedgy into the front seat of her car and trudged back through the snow to get the rest of her stuff. When she got back, Jeff and Hedgy, plus the box they were in were missing. She checked frantically all over the car interior and saw human footsteps that walked away from the car door where they were situated in their box. She leapt into investigation mode and followed the trail. It led to a house in the woods not far from the industrial estate she was working at. The footprints led her to the front door. She peered into the front window and could see no sign of life and no noise for any clues as to where Jeff and Hedgy were.

The man, built like a brick shit house carried Jeff and Hedgy into his four-wheeled truck and took off into the wilderness. After driving about twenty minute or so, he carried the box with Jeff and Hedgy in it and dumped it on the edge of a dense pine forest. Jeff and Hedgy felt the thud of the cardboard box go down. It hit the flaky snow and sunk half way. The man then went back to his car and simply left them to it. There were one or two other vehicles on the same road that almost rubbed out the tyre marks that left very little in the way of detection for Fran.

'Well, you did it again.'

'Did what?'

'You have obviously upset somebody, again.'

'Why me? Why not you? You have motive.'

'Motive, what motive? Why motive? For what motive?'

'Exactly, who have you upset, then?'

'Me. Meeee?'

'Yes you. What have you said? Or rather, what have you screeched?'

'Nobody, nothing. Why meee?'

'Have you, inadvertently bitten somebody?'

'No, no,no.'

'Well. What then?'

'I don't know.'

'Well, we've been dumped. Dumped in the middle of a forest with very dry and very cold stuff and its freezing my bollocks off.'

'It's iced snow if you must know, stupid.'

Jeff started to try to climb out of the box and said, 'It's far too cold in there.'

'Look, you'll freeze your bollocks off if you stay in that, so called iced white stuff.'

'Gently, watch out for me as well. I am still attached, contrary to my dreams, hopes, and fears. You are all I have to survive.'

'Yes and don't you forget it. You live on my prowess, pal.'

'Prowess, prowess? More like on the edge of your prowling for girls and sexual lustiness.'

'Ok, ok, give it a rest. You don't know what you are talking about. Those girls you talk about, want me, need me, crave for me, lust after me, and swoon to my every whim. Yes, and I think the white ice has frozen your probability cells along with your reality portions.'

'Don't you talk to me about portions? I am quite well endowed considering my stature, poise, and debonair masculinity. Those we saw earlier were boys' mere mortals of wanna be's. They are not in my universe and need more training to get to my absolute peakness.'

Jeff stood there stiff with muscular strength, proud-shafted protrusion, and sparkles in both eyes.

'Dream on, pal.'

A huge horse like animal bent down and sniffed around the box. Jeff and Hedgy managed to get back in the box in the nick of time and looked up at this Elk. Hedgy hissed as he did and the Elk became more intrigued. It sniffed Jeff's bollocks and Jeff tapped its nose with his bell end. On the intrusion, the Elk drew aback his nose and went in another time but this time aware that he needed to be careful because this creature could possibly bite. Hedgy looked up with snout forcibly pushed to the air and looked into the Elks light, sparkly, soft brown eyes. It had eyelashes the size of a long half-moon shaped comb. It fluttered them towards Hedgy and Hedgy hissed profusely with a dangerous warning noise.

The Elk looked to smile at Jeff sweetly and gave Jeff a sand paper lick on his shaft. Jeff wanted more. The roughness was so sensual, rough but tantalizingly tender. The experience felt like a rustic brush on his skin. Jeff got closer and tried to heighten his stance so that the Elk could get a more positive and direct spread of the tongue on his genitalia. It worked and Jeff was in seventh heaven. Jeff encouraged the Elk and tried to move even closer.

'Hey Conkers, what you doinx. I is waitinx for yous to plays wiv mees. Wheres yous bin?'

In a very low, deep, strong sexy voice, the Elk said, 'I found this container and there are some interesting pieces in it.'

Hedgy hissed again, and Jeff fell over because he lost his balance.

'Conkers, who's Conkers? Go away you oik.'

'He's is Conkers. Whos are yous?'

'None of your business. Bog off.'

'Conkers bitinx them. Conker nows.'

'I will do no such thing to inflict pain on anyone. Billy you should know that.'

'Theys is not friendlies. Theys is ferociating.'

'That is not even a word. You called Billy, then?'

'Uummmm, Billy no mates. You dangerouses. Conkers will bitinx yous if yous comes any closeness.'

'Ooohh I scared, shaking in my boots, in fact.'

'Goods, I is likes that.'

'We are not hostile, just cautious. Forgive him he knows not what he does.'

'Now I know why he's called Billy no mates. A bitch on heat or a dog not quite at its mental ability yet, perhaps?'

'Whats yous means? I is not mentals. I is all heres.'

'Yes and there, and here and definitely got problems. Go work them out and come back when you're a grown up.'

'Conkers bitinx him. He is vellys abusives to me's. Conkers!'

It was getting dark and the snow was turning grey but only with shade. A truck was moving on the snow road and heading their way. Jeff said, 'come on we had better move from here because we could get run over. Billy no mates ran off and hid away from the lights of a vehicle. The Elk just stood there like a statue. He did not move an antler or twitch an eyelid. He metaphorically speaking froze. The car was driven as close as she could to the Elk. Conkers still did not move a muscle. Fran got out of her car and went over to it. She wanted to check the Elk was all right. She also knew that the headlights of the car would make the Elk go into statue mode. The reasoning behind this is the Elk thought that, if he did not flinch, then nobody would see him there. Fran looked down and there in the box were her newfound friends. Billy no mates started barking and Fran quickly got Jeff, Hedgy and herself into the car. They drove off in a slow, wary fashion and dead slow.

JA, JA DU VARA PORRSTJÄRNOR

(YES, YES YOU BE PORN STAR)

It was dark when they got back and eeriness to the place. Silhouetted terrain covered in bulkiness. The snow disfigured the shadows and it looked in parts like distorted outlines of people or animals and then slight whispers of movement distantly teased. Fran got out the car when they arrived at her home and she carried them inside. She muttered an endearment in Swedish, then gave Hedgy a small bowl of milk followed by a biscuit treat. For once, it was comfort food, sweet and lovely. Early next morning, about five thirty a.m., Hedgy was given some muesli with milk, which he crunched at because he was ravenous. Anything was better than nothing and he did not know when he was going to be fed again.

When they got to the studio, Fran was confronted by one of the muscular men from yesterday. It looked to be some kind of confrontation.

"Vad har du förde dem tillbaka I henne för? ('What have you brought them back in her for?')

"Var det du som kidnappade dem, sedan övergett dem på älgarna skogen?"('Was it you who kidnapped them, then abandoned them in the Elks forest?')

"Tänk om det var? De är inte rätt? Det är sjukt att du har sex med en deformerad igelkott. "('What if it was? They're not right? It's sick you having sex with a deformed hedgehog.')

"Det är inte, det är bara annorlunda. Hur som helst Louise, säger vår regissör han vill ha honom i showen och vad han säger går. Ja, fick ett problem med det, se honom. "('It's not, it's just different. Anyway Louise, our director says he wants him in the show and what he says goes. Yes, got a problem with that, see him.')

With that, the muscular man stormed off.

Jeff was practicing his stance as he looked in a distant mirror. He told himself he was a very good catch for any lady. He also talked to himself, telling himself how gorgeous, debonair flair about his personality and everyone would adore him. He also reminisced Crete and thought he really could be a phallic symbol to the women of the world.

It took six months of heavy sexual encounters with the occasional petting from the other girls who wanted to play. One in particular (Gloria) would masturbate Jeff's torso, frequently. Gloria was his favourite, only because of the intensity of her desires.

With the film complete and the attention from the media that Jeff and Hedgy acclaimed, they found fame and frivolity but no fortune. Jeff was, in fact, a phallic symbol and he had his own website, fan club, and printed kisses on his bell end kissing the paper with Hedgy's paw print as well. Jeff and Hedgy were, without a dought PORN STARS in their own right.

"Vi ska på en liten resa och allt I din ära lilla Hedghog med ett huvud kamel puckel på ryggen." ('We are going on a little trip and its all in your honour little Hedghog with the one head camel hump on your back.')

'What did she say?'

'No worries, its just gobbledy gook again.'

'Why do they always do that?'

'Do what?'

'Talk in their own gobbledy gook instead of English, like us?'

'To be honest, I don't even think we speak any language, let alone English. All languages are a combination of others anyway.'

'True, true.'

'Anyway, no human has ever really listened to us or understood what we are trying to say.'

'They understood your shriek and Billy no mates, the other day.'

'Yes but, that was not a language as such. It was just to get their attention.'

'Well the shrieking and hissing gobbledy gook worked for them, anyway.'

Fran carried on with, "du är både kända och jag är stolt över att känna dig." ('you are both famous and I am proud to know you.')

She started to chuckle, "ni har gett mig personligen, sådan glädje och det är kul att jobba med dig. Hantz har stora planer för oss när vi kommer tillbaka från Soho, London. "('you have given me personally, such pleasure and it is fun working with you. Hantz has big plans for us when we get back from Soho, London.')

'I know that place.'

Jeff and Hedgy started singing, It's coming home, It's coming home (Three Lions).

Fran heard all the kerfuffling and put Hedgy and Jeff into their usual box, and then left them in the corner of her bedroom. Before she left, she emptied a packet of cheese and onion crisps over the box and onto their bodies. Hedgy was elated and tried to munch as they fell onto his nose and head.

The day had come for their red carpet excursion. Jeff and Hedgy had bubble bath treatments and were spruced for their organized adventure, for a change. Their cardboard box was turned into a wooden, pull along behind you, trolley. It had wheels, a fluffy red blanket, and a huge light creamy sky blue pillow that covered the bottom of the cart. Fran put them in to see what they looked like and was over the moon with her findings. Hedgy thought it weird, bouncy and had problems balancing on the foam pillow. Once he spread his weight and feet, then flounce for comfort, he settled in quite well. Jeff just went with the flow.

Night came and so did the cold. Their old box was not very weather proof and the chills bit them in a few sensitive areas. Fran wrapped them up in a furry synthetic cream blanket and went to bed herself.

'Thank god for the blanket.'

'D'you think we're off tomorrow then?'

'Well, from what I can tell and my expert observations, I don't bloody well know.'

'Why can't we just hold a civilized conversation for once? You're always on the defensive.'

'Me, me, what about you. You are sarcastic most of the time. Laugh at me the rest and ignore me when I need you most. So tell me pal, what part of civilised do you want, then?'

'The part that says, you like me, loves me, want me as your friend, and companion. I'm lonely with a thing I struggle to be friends with most of the time but mostly, something I have literally got attached to.'

'Oohh my giddy aunt, don't go soft on me. Are you ill?'

'There you go again. Civilised, do you know what civilised is?'

'Ummm yes, be polite and boring.'

'No, you knit whit, it means be nice, thoughtful, caring, be good to others as they are to you.'

'And?'

'My point being just be courteous, kind and friendly.'

'I can't be doing with all that. Look take me as I am or not at all.'

'You're horrid. The most horridist thing that went to the planet horrid. Good night. Hope all the bed bugs bite and you have all your nightmares in the next sleepless sleep.'

'Ooh don't be like that. I was only joking. Hedgy, Hedgy?'

'Shut the fuck up. I get the message. Nothing changes; you just drone, snore, and drop dead.'

'Jeff began to listen at the end but his pride got in the way and he just did as he was told and settled down to sleep.'

Hedgy snored his head off as usual. He sounded as if his sinuses were blocking his whole bodies and not just his breathing. He was just so loud. Jeff found the noise intolerable but dare not wake the poor critter. After all, he had already upset him and made him very sad and angry.

Jeff, exhausted drifted into a nightmare.

His dream got to be intense and he could see Hedgy in the distance. They were apart for the first time and Jeff was devastated. He was so used to Hedgy carrying him everywhere and doing everything for him. In the nightmare, they had just escaped and found themselves in the industrial car park just outside the studio. They ran for cover and then when the coast was clear started walking. After a two and a half hour stroll, he could see what looked like a truck stop parking area. Warehouses and possibly an industrial estate surrounded it.

Hedgy climbed underneath one of the juggernauts and settled into the rear axle. Jeff asked if he could join him. Hedgy said, 'no find your own way home. I'm off.'

'But Hedgy we've done everything together. You're my mate. Come on move over. We can escape together.'

'No, shove off.'

Jeff, with frozen bollocks in the snow, limped away with a destroyed friendship in tow.

As he did so, an Indian man with a thick coat and a heavy turban on his head pulled himself into the cab. Jeff realised that if the lorry moved and where Hedgy was situated, he would definitely be squished to a pulp. Jeff tried to run back and save his friend but the screams from Hedgy went through Jeff's whole being. Tears came to his eyes and he almost felt his pain. Hedgy had been killed outright and torn in half by the mechanics of the lorry parts. Mechanical objects have no feelings and just did what they were told.

Jeff went over to a pool of hedgehog blood and guts that spilled under the Lorries under carriage. The Indian man went to have a look at what the noise was all about and he felt the disgust of hurting another creature. He was mentally and physically sick to see all that blood and gore. At the same time he never noticed Jeff hiding behind one of the wheels trying not to cry out loud with contempt for the driver that had just run over part of his life, his friend, companion and most of all his brother in so many historical adventures that they did together. At that point, Jeff did not care that his bollocks had frostbite and that the cold was gnawing at his shaft. He wanted to die with his soul mate, pal, bestist friend in the whole wide world but another lorry pulled up and just missed Jeff by inches. He knew that he had to get home alone and staggered away with the occasional glance of tears back at his mutilated body, dead, and nothingness left.

Jeff gulped with a very dry throat. He found himself not being able to breath and calling out in his sleep, which eventually woke himself up. He found a very silent, calm room with no movement except Hedgy snoring so loudly that the noise was so inviting to Jeff. He looked around and could not believe that nobody had heard his screams or cries for help. The room was how he left it before going to sleep. Hedgy was in a deep sleep and, yes, he was alive. Jeff cried even more the tears from his dreams overflowed to reality. He did not care. He looked at Hedgy, as a parent would to a new born baby, with admiration, adoringly proud and just the thought of being part of something so special. He was so happy to see his little mate still attached, healthy, and breathing. Jeff realised how much he really did love him. He also knew he would not want to live without his special friend, HEDGY.

Fran came in at around five a.m. She was bright eyed and had a healthy bouncy, personality that alerted all who pervade her happiness. The first thing she did was smile at Jeff and Hedgy, spoke something endearing in Swedish and kissed Jeff on his knob. Jeff was awake but not in. Hedgy was awake nearly with a sluggish temperament and felt all this happiness a little too much for that time of the morning. They both needed a little understanding as to the hour at which they had just abruptly been woken up and the fact they had not slept very well.

Hedgy was plonked on the table whilst Jeff tried to go back to sleep on his back. Muesli was set before him. It was bits of fruit, grains, and covered with fresh creamy milk. Hedgy sucked up the milk with his snout and chomped on the occasional fruit but the grains got stuck in his minute teeth. After breakfast, Fran nudged Jeff and she cleared and washed the breakfast things. Her suitcase was brought out from her bedroom along with her bag.

'Well, from the looks of it, I think we're off on our travels.'

Jeff jolted as he heard Hedgy speak, 'D'you think this is the trip to Soho, London.'

'Uummm, I hope so. I want to go home.'

'Me too but to Soho? I don't know that neck of the woods. D'you?'

'I've heard of it and I know its England but no, I don't know. Now stay perfectly still. I am tired and am going back to sleep.'

'Oh come on Jeff. There's no time for that now. Wakey, wakey, rise and shine.'

'Good night, sleep tight and hope the bedbugs don't bight. Snort, snort.'

Jeff leaned his body over to one side and started to doze. Fran came in and hit the tip of his knob, said something in Swedish like wake up, rise and shine, then went back into the bathroom to comb her hair.

'What was that for?'

Jeff, you need to wake up and stay alert. We will be on the move shortly.'

'How short?'

'I don't know three inches or so. Look how am I supposed to know. Just bloody wake up. You know, jolly up and hey ho, here we go.'

'I have not got a go in my body parts.'

'Yes, I've noticed, you cretinous klutz.'

'Look, leave the big words to me. You know nothing.'

Jeff swade with one eye open, searching for Fran. They heard a knock on the door and they were off. The camera crew came in and took all the luggage that was Fran's and other stuff that was stored at hers overnight. Mr Muscly grinned profusely at Jeff and Hedgy whilst negotiating their passage and then seating arrangements in the four by four truck. It did not take long to load up and get on their way.

Jeff said to Hedgy, 'can I sleep now?'

Hedgy replied, 'go on then but lean to the right.'

It did not take them long to travel to the airport. As they waited for their flight, Fran went window shopping in the duty free and the men patrolled the luggage area. Jeff and Hedgy were taken to another part of the airport to be boarded with other pets.

From the time of boarding the aeroplane to landing in London, it took roughly two and a half hours. Jeff and Hedgy travelled in an open crate and were made very comfortable. The journey was too easy. The ride non-consequential. At the other end however, questions had to be answered as to what Jeff and Hedgy were. This was found to be most difficult indeed as Fran, especially did not have all the answers. After a few hours in the airport, they were told it was all right to leave. Fran thought this strange but found out because of the publicity Jeff and Hedgy got that made the questioning an understanding of their role in all this and they were able to get into the country. Therefore, in other words their reputation preceded them. What a stroke of luck.

Everyone in the party was jet lagged, even though the journey was not that long it still affected everybody's equilibrium.

Finally, they arrived at the Blomsberry Hotel, Soho, London. It was simply the best, gorgeous. In fact, Fran said it was amazing. Fran arranged to have something to eat in her room as she booked herself and the rest of the party into their rooms. They were all put on the third floor and their rooms were next door to each other. Mr Muscly carried Jeff and Hedgy in their new pull along carriage. When the room was opened, Fran gasped in awe of how designer everything looked. She was in creative heaven and revelled in palatial. Mr Muscly put Jeff and Hedgy next to the huge settee and said something in Swedish to Fran then left. Fran answered only half listening. She quickly got up and picked Jeff up by his shaft and walked into the spacious bedroom, where there was a bed so big it could get at least four people in it, across. She carried on walking past the bed and in the corner was a cot. It was luxurious. All wood, varnished and had butterflies dancing on a mobile above it. The bed linen matched the purple, pink, blue, and green butterfly colours. The background was of creams, lemons, browns and deep blues that had all run into each other, like ink spills. She left them there to get used to their new surroundings.

'Well this is nice. All baby coo coo, dummy sucking, nappy squelching, and small sticked night horrored bed.'

'Well, its better than that monstrosity of a pull me push you shoe box, thing.'

'I happen to like our new transport, thank you very much.'

'What those ridiculous dolls prams push along? You must be joking.'

'No I'm not. It's great when you can see over the top but then again I'm the Porn Star. They don't need to see you. So, I will be on full display in my carriage. Head held high and phallic to drool over.'

'Oh give me a break. You are so full of bullshit. Phallic my arse, penis more like.'

'Do you know what phallic means, stupid?'

'Dick symbol, I guess.'

'No it means all the women are going to want to touch, grope, and feel my undivided greatness.'

'Undivided, huh? Yeah right. Undivided crap more like.'

'Look, I know you are jealous but they need to see my individuality and that cart will show me off to perfection.'

'You are so full of yourself.'

'Of course. They lust after me, want me, and need my presence.'

'Look, just go get a life, and shut the fuck up, please.'

The door flew open and the director stormed in. His presence look to be a practice run for the red carpet scenario. He was dressed in his suave draped over coat that looked two sizes too big and leather trousers. He looked loud and slutty. For a bloke he looked as if he wanted to be sixteen again but looked sixty-ish. His parted hair was thin and grey and his sunglasses were very inappropriate for what he was trying to portray. Fran turned abruptly, looked at his masquerade, and change her face to look the part of; it is the important director with the big wallet of money and fortune at every street corner. She wanted riches beyond her wildest dreams and a career to make money fast.

'Look what the cat dragged in.'

'Oh yeah, Evel Knievel look alike.'

'No stupid. The Director, Hantz.'

'I know, stupid.'

Fran poured him a drink from her drinks cabinet and put some ice in his Jack Daniels. He went to sit with his coat still wrapped around his shoulders and spilt his drink. Fran quickly found some toilet tissue from the bathroom and mopped it up. He carried on with his famous big I am, flagrant, arrogance, and carried on talking in Swedish to Fran. The conversation was intense and it sounded as if he were giving her instruction along with orders of the film festival planning.

As quick as the Director came, then he went. Fran tucked Hedgy and Jeff into their vehicle with their new blanket, turned off the lights, said something in Swedish with a smile and went to bed.

A telephone rang in the lounge. It was very early morning, about five or even earlier. It woke Jeff and Hedgy up. Fran rushed into where they were and carried Jeff and Hedgy into the bathroom. The sink had been filled and bubble bath spilled all over the surfaces. It stank of lavender. Jeff and Hedgy were immersed and the warmth was comforting after waking so abruptly. Hedgy could feel the bubbles rising up into his nose and did a twitchy sneeze. Jeff, on the other hand, felt the bubbles around his bollocks but very little else. Hedgy had all the water.

'Hey you? Wash me as well. These bubbles are getting cold.'

Hedgy just made a heart-warming, uummmmmm lovally.'

Fran flipped Hedgy onto his side and soaked Jeff's body in the relaxing warm water.

'Arrrhh, oooooh, arrh, niccccccce.'

Hedgy, on the other hand, was simply drowning.

'Cough, splutter, helllllllp. Cough, cough, spit. Hey Jefff, spit, cough?'

'Arrh, this is lovely and warm.'

'Jefff, cough, splutter. Jeff, cough splutter, choke, helllllllp.'

Jeff was so engrossed in his newfound luxurious bubble bath that he did not want to move but his friend was calling. He decided to try to push himself around so that Hedgy could breath.

Fran realised that there was something wrong as Hedgy had gone under. Jeff by this time was trying to sway back and forth to save his friend in desperation. Fran grasped Jeff's shaft and pulled them both out, instantly.

Hedgy was limp and Jeff was wilting. Jeff could not live without him. What ever happened to Hedgy, obviously affected Jeff, big time? Fran panicked and shook them vigorously, adding some worried Swedish words like, "vaknar, andetag, öppna ögonen, kom igen, vi har inte tid för det här, och sluta fumla runt." ('Wake up, breath, open your eyes, come on, we have not time for this, and stop messing about.')

Hedgy coughed, spluttered, and projectile vomited, water. Jeff's eyes opened but his body was in shutdown. He was limper than a limpet that had no rocks to muscle on with other limpets.

Fran was so relieved that something like a cough told her Hedgy was alive and kicking. Hedgy got the coughing out of the way and hissed profusely.

'What the ruddy hell are you trying to do to me woman?'

'You all right, Hedgy? Hedgy? Hedgy, answer me.'

'Yes, yes, but only just. That demented woman is trying to drown me.'

'She has also just this minute, saved you.'

'So, shut the fuck up.'

When Hedgy said those endearing words, Jeff knew he was back to nearly being himself again. Fran quickly got a towel and dried them both. Fran put a multi-coloured bow tie and tied it to the middle of Jeff's shaft. It was not too tight and it felt quite comfortable.

When Fran had finished preparing the Porn Stars for their debut, she placed them in the new four-wheel pull along truck. Now they were all calmed, wrapped with tranquillity and so looking forward to their forthcoming adventures.

Fran dressed for seduction, with a little pink number. Her pink, stiletto shoes were dangerously high. In fact, suicidal if she were to fall.

The phone rang again. This time she answered it, spoke in Swedish, collected her fluffy, white, false fur chest coat, handbag, and picked up the trolley arm. She pulled Jeff and Hedgy's vehicle out of her hotel room, down the corridor to the nearest lift. Fran saw Mr Muscly come out of his room, close and lock his door, then knock the cameraman's door. Fran carried on and pulled Jeff and Hedgy's vehicle into the lift and pressed to go down.

They all met up in the lobby. After half an hour or so a Rolls Royce Phantom convertible, in a soft white colour pulled up in front of the steps of the Hotel waiting for its guests to depart. Mr Muscle picked up Jeff and Hedgy's vehicle and placed them high on the back of the seat so that their public could see Jeff clearly. This was difficult but achievable all the same. Fran sat closely to them as their guardian angels. From the incident earlier in, the day she was determined that nothing else was going to happen to her friends again.

The cameraman sat on the other side in the back. The Director sat at the front with the driver and some other relatives and friends filled the other seats.

It did not take them long to get to the red carpeted venue, festival. The Director stepped out to the crowd firstly. There was plenty of applause. Then, the family and friends. Mr Muscly got a few whistles and extra claps with some women trying to touch him but only if they got close enough. They liked him obviously. The cameraman was hiding as usual, behind his camera, mainly because he was very shy. He liked it that way. A security guard came and helped Fran carry Jeff and Hedgy out of the Rolls Royce.

The audience went ballistic. They saw Jeff in the air and screamed. Suddenly the security guard called for assistance on his walky talky. The crowd was closing in and the barriers were shaking with the pressure of people clambering to get to Jeff. Luckily, once on the red carpet the barriers were placed in a much more spacious position. The crowd roared with excitement. Hedgy grinned from whisker to whisker and Jeff's eyes were shiny bright with awesomeness Flashing camera lights sparkled their ambient glares. As they walked through the atmosphere was electric. Jeff had found his phallic fame again. He, at last revelled in everyone loving his presence and felt like a god that nobody could touch.

Hedgy, on the other hand liked the lime light and the attention but knew the attention was for Jeff and any attention given was bounced off his charm and centred on Jeff the magnificent.

Jeff bowed his bell end and squashed his bow tie, often at anyone staring for his attention. The entrance of the building was upon them. Jeff and Hedgy were quickly ushered away to a small room. Fran followed after handing out promotional literature with Jeff and Hedgy's photograph's on to the public.

The changing room was, to say the least grotty. There were no windows and the carpet was filthy with fag ends, bits of thread and ground in bits of food. Water stains all over. Looking on the outside, then into the building it looked so classy, elegant, and super dooper clean and healthy. Nevertheless, to come to a dingy, box hovel, was such a pity. Fran left Jeff and Hedgy in the vehicle and went to find out what she was to do next.

'Wow, what a day. Fame is brilliant don't you think. All those women swooning.'

'That's all I get from you women, women, women.'

'Well, what do you expect? Women of pleasure are my life, now. I want to please them, wooo them, charm the knickers off them.'

'Can't you think of anything else, like where's lunch, snacks, drink or something yummy to chew on?'

'This room hums of filth.'

Fran came back in the nick of time. She grabbed the trolley arm and manoeuvred it through the door. Mr Muscly took the reins and pulled the trolley through some of the other corridors and eventually, through to the back way that ended up through the door to the bottom of the stage where they were applauded on entry. Everybody eventually stopped making any noise and settled into waiting time. Five minutes later, the lights dimmed. The film started and so did shuffling. People were fidgeting for a more cosy position, ready for the big event.

The Director had a reputation for success. It was felt that this film was already a brilliant success because of this.

The movie was long and loud. Far too loud for Hedgy because they were put close up to the speakers. It seemed the movie went on for hours. Jeff was almost embarrassed to see his action from a public point of view. He twisted and looked around, the room at all the fascinating faces as their eyes were mesmerised by their sexual acts being performed right in front of everybody. Jeff was taken aback and it made him think about how raw it all became. It also dawned on him the amount of shagging he had to endure for, in some cases, minute acting time he had to undertake for a short part of the movie. Nevertheless, Jeff was in a vast amount of parts, which made him an active hero.

Porn Star gratitude came at the end of the film. Each actor stood up and was applauded according to greatness. When Jeff was announced, it became more apparent of his greatness with a standing ovation, whistling, hip hopping, and crying. The girls just loved him. Jeff was their sexual hero and god. A sex partner everybody wanted.

ACCIDENTS DO HAPPEN

The Festival Director walked to centre stage and people were asked to calm down and then sit down. The Festival was not over and speeches were to be celebrated. The Director won last year and was called to the stage to be given yet another celebratory trophy for his mantelpiece. He was very happy to be centre stage and shook the hand of the Festival Director, said a long-winded speech with applause after as he walked off stage. The director after roughly twenty minutes turned to Jeff and told him he had won actor of the year and the sexiest thing they had ever seen award. Fran and Mr Muscly carried Jeff and Hedgy to centre stage to collect his award. Hedgy hissed with anger, jealousy, and downright aggressiveness at his crowd of Jeff lovers. The Director on stage handing out the awards laughed and made a joke of Hedgy's hissing. He handed the award to Fran who accepted on Jeff's behalf. She also gave a little speech but with English subtitles already prepared on the screen for just this particular occasion. After her speech, she was applauded and then Jeff was screamed at, applauded heavily and women were fainting in front of him as he was carried off stage. The security guards were very prepared and cleared the isle of bodies. Some needed medical attention and so the St.

John's Ambulance Brigade that was volunteers for these occasions sped into their specialist action.

The director, cameraman and family, plus friends were hurried to a waiting area. Then they were joined a few minutes later by Jeff, Hedgy, Fran, and Mr Muscly and instantly taken to the Rolls Royce Phantom parked at the back of the building for their escape back to the Hotel Blomsberry. Waiting for them were more screaming women at the entrance. The Hotel Manager had arranged for the Porn Star party to go around to the back entrance, where a room had been prepared especially for their entertainment.

Jeff was bursting with exertion and swayed his body to the music. Hedgy tried to keep in sync but it was difficult.

'Hey how ya doin dude?'

'Jeff, they can't hear you.'

'How's it grooving dude?'

'Jeff they can't hear a dam thing you are saying.'

'Hey give a Porn Star a Champagne cocktail, dude?'

'Jeff, Jeff?'

'What dude?'

'Shut the fuck up, pal. You're doing my head in.'

'I am enjoying myself. Ooooooh look Can Can girlies. Hedgy git your ass over there. I want to watch them sassy lassies.'

Hedgy took no notice but Jeff was trying to forcibly push him towards the dancing girls.

'Hey, hey, pal. This way. Follow me, right now, pal.'

Jeff was determined to go have a look closer to those voluptuous, gorgeous females.

Hedgy spotted food, tables of the stuff. His favourite, snails, delicious, succulent, mouth-watering snails in butter and something else. Hedgy followed his nose but Jeff followed his lust. Both were fighting against each other but nobody won and neither had the stamina to forcibly pull harder than the other did.

'Ok you follow me. I need food or you will die.'

'Well nah, you follow me or I will hit you hard with my manly weapon and kill you if you don't go over to them there Can Can girlies. Look over there.'

'Jeff just give me five to eat and then we go get your Can Can girlies.'

'No now, Hedgy, I need to go right this minute.'

'No.'

'Yes.'

'No.'

'Yes.'

Fran came over and plonked Hedgy on the table by the snails. Jeff bent over and they fell off the table. Fran caught them in the nick of time as always. She told Mr Muscly to feed Hedgy the snails while she went to talk to someone else. He obliged.

'I knew it. Fran loves me. I always knew it really.'

'Just hurry up they're going to stop dancing in a minute. Come on snail race, just swallow. No chewing.'

'Jeff?'

'I know, shut the fuck up.'

'You said it, pal.'

Mr Muscly was getting fed up with serving Hedgy. He put them on the floor and walked off.

'Free, run.'

'No run. Girlies, that way over there, Hedgy, over that way.'

Fran captured their freedom and made a beeline for their intentions. She swooped them up in her arms and carried them to her newfound table. She sat Hedgy on it and started to feed him some very expensive champagne by the glass. Hedgy found he liked the stuff and guzzled. Fran was laughing at the shear mouthfuls of intoxicating liquor that Hedgy was consuming. She could hardly hold and tilt the glass fast enough for his pleasure.

Everyone celebrated with loads of champagne and canopies. The drunken state of everyone was amidst the best of them. The night sky was young and shone over the ambience of all who wanted. The night air was warm and inviting. Fran got hold of Jeff's shaft, thinking it was another bottles of champers, and then dropped them on the floor beside herself. She laughed and thought nothing of Hedgy and Jeff on the floor, then reached for another bottle from the middle of the table.

Hedgy was drunk. Jeff swayed freely to the motion of Hedgy's gait. They staggered to what looked like a burger lying lonely and un eaten in the road. Hedgy focused on his absolute favourite food of all time and bent according to the view of the prospective gastric delights. There was a sound of screeching brakes as Jeff Cousins tries to take evasive action to miss the object that had just stepped in front of his moving car.

Jeff Cousins loved his new London office. He travelled to and from Berkshire every working day. He swerved across the road and his car careered into a lamppost. For the second time in his life, he could see his world ebbing away. Hedgy and Jeff were torn apart, separated by the impact. Hedgy curled up tightly into a little ball in the gutter and Jeff had been flung to the opposite pavement alongside the wrecked vehicle.

Paramedics and the fire brigade were quickly at the scene and when the Police arrived they cordoned off the area. Jeff Cousin's blooded body was removed from the wreckage and placed in the back of the ambulance. Flashing lights raced all over the place. Panic was all around. People sobered up immediately. Fran saw the ambulance dancing lights and thought there was more surprises install for that night that she did not know about and embraced the ambience until she saw the ambulance and police car. Every spectator was stunned and stood in their tracks not knowing what to say or do. The heavy quietness, stunned lookers on. Nobody thought of Hedgy or Jeff. They just saw Jeff Cousins in the back of the ambulance ready to be taken to hospital.

Jeff the Maverick Penis was spotted by a police officer when taping off the area.

'There's a cock down here. Whose is it?'

Hedgy was shaken but not viably harmed. He scuttled off into the undergrowth and found himself in the local park.

When they got to hospital, blood tests were done and it proved that the penis found was, in fact Jeff Cousins own little friend. They managed to do emergency surgery and sewed it back in its rightful place. Did it work? Only time will tell that story. Was Jeff happy to be back? His memory was wiped and had no recollection of any of his past with Hedgy. He was plain and simply a pissing, wanking, sexual pleasure toy again. He could not think, answer back, or even make comments of disgust or admiration. He just flopped and Jeff Cousins waited for any sign of feeling such as blood flow, erectional function, warm urine dispersal, and tenderness as in sensitivity.

As for Hedgy, he missed the weight on his back and found it difficult to walk without gauging his stance for manoeuvrability. He hid away from anything that moved, animal, vegetable and mineral. He was in a place, on his own, stuck with no companionship and petrified he might be caught by humanoids. In time, he also acknowledged that he was free. Free from moaning, nagging, and abuse. He missed Jeff and all his ways of getting on Hedgy's nerves. Jeff entertained him, showed him the way, and got him out of so many scrapes with his quick thinking. How was he going to live without his bestist friend in the whole wide world? In time, he learned to get along and get on with his life but it was not easy. He had spent too much time with an entity that took over his whole being, only to be cast away by a stupid car. He eventually learnt to live alone again and interact with other creatures in the park. He met a female Hedgehog. Arhh but that's another story, chuckle, chuckle!

ACKNOWLEDGEMENTS

Thank you to my sister Caron Lunn for letting me use her chuhauha's name 'Rocky' for my cause.

Richard Ingram has helped me with my flight from Germany to Japan. Thanks Rich, much appreciated.

Sam, Carol Ingram's dog has helped me out by using one of his many names and his character to create, Sammy No nutts. Woof! Woof!

Ann Hunt, my beautiful aunty gave me chufta, chufta. I had never heard that word before, and so she is to blame lol. She really is one special, gorgeous lady and I love her to bits.

My niece Maxine Hunt is to blame for so many things in this book. In addition, she plays a cruel game of UNO ha, ha, ha. Love you Max xxxx

Jane Bonsignore has given me permission to use her dog's name Billy no mates for one of my characters and a Woofy thank you to you Billy!

I would like to thank Fiona Allen for helping me.

I would like to thank Martin Drakeford and Josh Carvell for helping with suggesting the Rolls Royce Phantom in a soft white colour. Brilliant.

Sarah Payne for being such a great neighbour.

I would like to thank Nigel Payne for his phallic symbol that lights up at night in his back garden. This gave me inspiration, chuckle, chuckle.

I would like to thank Treeve Sperrin and his family at The Lord Nelson pub and restaurant for helping me in my quest.

Thanks to Pete Hulme from the Weddington Social Club for all his help, much appreciated.

Thanks to Chris Peers for all his help.

ILLUSTRATIONS

All illustrations designed and created
By the author
JAYNE BELINDA ALLEN